THE NEON REVELATION

TT MADDEN

TIMBER GHOST PRESS

The Neon Revelation

Published by Timber Ghost Press

Printed in the United States of America

Edited by: Beverly Bernard

Cover Art and Design by: Don Noble

Interior Design: Timber Ghost Press

Print ISBN: 979-8-9925767-2-6

www.TimberGhostPress.com

Also by the Author:
The Familialists
The Cosmic Color
Student Bodies
Gorman's House
places where you cannot be: an afro-american travel guide

CONTENT WARNINGS

This book contains mentions of sexual assault, miscarriage, and death during childbirth, as well as depictions of religious nationalism, racism, misogyny, transphobia, supernatural impregnation and childbirth, and gun violence.

For every queer who finds themselves in a hostile land.

CONTENTS

1: PROFANE

PART I:

DESECRATION

"If—what is it—half of all women poop during childbirth," Nico asked, "do you think Mary shit herself when she gave birth to Jesus?"

HEAVEN ON EARTH

Roan thinks about what people say someone is supposed to feel when they enter heaven and guesses that's the aesthetic this place is going for—grand and welcoming, a view of the Midwest plains, with the simplicity of endless shrubs and low, rolling hills, crop fields in the distance, the few buildings that dot the landscape shouting distance from one another. A Manifest Destiny vibe. Having grown up in various two-bedroom apartments, floors often packed with families, it's hard for her to imagine anyone having all this property to themselves, and she guesses that's America in a nutshell.

There are huge gates marking the entrance to the property with a carved, wooden sign above them decreeing the name of the place as COLUMBIA. It's different from the rest of the town of Parthas, a quiet little valley far lusher and greener than the rest of the Nevada landscape Roan witnessed on her journey so far.

She knows the people here claim the greenery, the oasis, as she's often heard it called, as another one of Columbia's supposed miracles. During Roan's research into the place, she found the miracles to be of the bog-standard Catholic variety: weeping statues, visions of the Virgin Mary, and impressive if unsubstantiated reports of miraculous healing. But even if they were true, Roan knows she can't count on a miracle for what she's there to do. She's got only herself, especially now.

There is an archway but no fence, at least not at this part of the property. Roan guesses that's what the cowboys are for. Flanking the arch are half a dozen men on horseback, scattered about and posturing as they watch the small crowd walk up from Parthas proper and through the gates of Columbia. Were it not for the modern weaponry, the bulletproof vests, the walkie-talkies, and cell phones clipped to their belts, they would have looked plucked right out of a classic Western.

It all reminds Roan of an attempt to return to a place that never really existed and was only ever a fantasy in the heads of men nostalgic for a time in which they never lived, in which they could have even more power than they already do. Even Roan has to admit that parts of that fantasy are occasionally enticing, like the warm summer wind rolling through the plains, making the grass look like a green sea. For a moment, she tells herself it's okay to believe its promise, that this place and the miracles its people have been claiming are all real.

But then she remembers Nico. Remembers why she's here. Remembers that none of these people would want her because of what she is.

To the people that come on pilgrimages to Columbia, to the crowd that surrounds her as they walk through the gates, death must be something beautiful, something that, while they try to avoid it, they ultimately don't resist too hard when it comes. Because for them it's not the end. Not like it was for Nico. Not like Nico's end was an ending of Roan's own.

Those who've never suffered much say there's a redemptive value in suffering. Roan can't believe that. There's no world in which the kind of pain she's witnessed, the kind of pain she carries, means anything good.

Roan wonders if any of these people have experienced real death, if they've ever seen it up close, looked it in the eye. She can't believe they have. Death isn't like how they show it in movies. The henchman doesn't double over bloodless at the mere sound and muzzle flash of the hero's gunshot. No, he hits the ground holding his spilling guts, leaking snot and tears and crying for his mommy, and he finally shits and pisses himself when he goes, several painful minutes or hours later.

Roan's never gone to Nico's grave, never visited her in the rain or the dark or even the snow like she would in a movie, because Nico's not really in the ground there. There's just meat and bone in the slowly decaying shape of Nico.

She doesn't even know if Nico's child has a separate grave marker.

She doesn't suppose that matters either, because whoever they were and whoever they were going to be is gone too, just like their mother, and Roan is alone now.

Roan does not look like—and, in fact, is not—the kind of person this churchgoing crowd thinks of when they think about heaven. Plenty of men have told her she's far too muscular for a woman and then have wondered if she was a *real* woman, then immediately jumped to conclusions and then bigotry—and occasionally violence—when they decided, *yeah, she's gotta be a tranny*. She's already seen the people around her staring wide-eyed at her mass, her tattoos, wondering if they've clocked her yet as *one of those transsexuals*. How many transvestigators are in the crowd looking at her throat or her hips or the width of her shoulders or her crotch where there is no bulge because she has had her bottom surgery, but nothing is ever good enough for those people?

The tattoos all across her body don't distract the onlookers from the heresy of her existence. Surely, they make her even more of a degenerate. After all, they're not just a couple of small, tasteful ones on the shoulder or the inside of the wrist or below the collarbone like she's seen a couple of the other approaching women bear. No, Roan is *covered,* with sleeves on both arms going down to the backs of her hands and on her tank-top-exposed chest. If they could see her legs and feet beyond her jeans and Doc Martens, they'd see she's inked down there too, on her stomach, her back. The tattoos are of snakes, bats, shining supernovas, and cathedral spires, of beautiful, naked mermaids and Jolly Rogers and mythical creatures. She's not a single, matching piece but dozens of images put together, crowding up the canvas of her skin. Her long, purple-streaked hair is pulled back into a ponytail, and through her purple-shaded eyes, with her lips pursed and dark, she sees everyone trying not to watch her. She wonders if the people who ogle her think she's a reformed Satanist or someone who wants to detransition, a boy who was brainwashed into thinking he was a girl, who perhaps escaped a cult or some equally dangerous queers, and is now on the path to salvation and to return to who God made him.

What do they mean? an elderly woman once asked her, staring at her exposed, ink-covered arms while Roan bagged her groceries during the few months she worked at a MacReady's grocery store.

They don't mean anything. They're fuckin' cool, she'd said. She'd expected resistance, for the woman to offer some sort of critique of an entire generation based on the unknown decisions of a single woman (who this old gal had not, in fact, clocked. Roan wasn't sure if this old woman even knew of the existence of trans people at all), but instead of resistance, Roan saw something in the old bird's eyes she didn't expect: a wistfulness, a longing. Like the woman wished she could be that free, wished she could have had the strength to live like Roan did. *You know,* Roan said, *a flash tattoo from this place down the street will only cost you about eighty bucks.* She "forgot" to ring up her last three bags, all with the woman's most expensive items. She wonders if the woman ever went and got one and hopes she did.

That's another thing. While Roan does not look like the kind of person this churchgoing, miracle-witnessing crowd thinks of when they think about heaven, neither does she behave that way. Because she's not there for salvation.

She's there to kill a man.

Roan first heard the name Andrew Garrett whispered with what sounded like reverence, calmly slithering from between Nico's lips. It was a name that meant something good because she'd fallen for him, and then a name that conjured rage because of what he'd done to her, and then a name with so many mixed feelings she could never disentangle because it was responsible for the little pink lines on the pregnancy test Nico held in shaky hands as she sat on their bathroom floor. After a time, it was a name that meant nothing because there was going to be no Andrew Garrett, only Roan and Nico and the little one growing in her belly.

But now it's a name that means everything because it's all Roan has left.

Roan knows that in the story the patrons of Columbia will tell about this event years from now, she will be the villain—the dangerous foreigner infiltrating their idyllic society. Come to corrupt. Come to kill. They had a place that was literally granting them miracles, and the most despicable kind of person came from the outside and destroyed it. But she doesn't care about the future's history. Her own future is gone, and all she has left is history. Her desire is to make someone hurt for the hurt inflicted upon her, to fist-fuck a world that is empty on true justice while the little devil on her shoulder laughs with delight.

Roan doesn't know if this is where the concept first showed up, but she always associates it with Looney Tunes—a tiny version of yourself dressed like an angel on one shoulder, and another version dressed like a devil on the other. She's sure there's got to be some religious significance to which side the little homunculi are on, but she has no clue. The closest she's ever come to Catholicism is wearing a schoolgirl uniform a size too small, pretending to do homework out of a ratty, moth-eaten, 1990s physics textbook. A man who frequented the bar she worked at after she got fired from the grocery store (for "forgetting" to ring up bags) paid her two hundred dollars a session to "tutor" her, the pretense of foreplay. She knew almost all of the answers, but she deliberately marked most of them incorrectly because she wanted another paddle for every answer she got wrong. She wanted him to hit her again, to find it hard to sit down later, her ass-cheeks stinging, the echo of the pain forbidding her from doing so. When he finally hiked up her skirt and fucked her in the ass, because it was the only hole she had at the time, she could hear him muttering Hail Marys in between his needy, quaking thrusts.

But despite the cartoonery, she visualizes it, the tiny, devilish Roan on her shoulder, all red onesie and fishnet tights and high heels and leather straps, the pitchfork balanced across her shoulders, invisible to everyone else as she follows the crowd through Columbia's gates, the place of these alleged miracles.

One of the cowboys leads the way, and from where they crest the top of the hill, Roan can see down into the rest of the valley. There's a large farmhouse with a flagpole out front that bears a menagerie of flags; the stars and stripes, the Nevada state flag, the Thin Blue Line, and Don't Tread On Me. But there's also one with a white background and a black cross formed out of two horizontal lines and two vertical lines, all the edges sharp, as if bladed. Before the cross is a simple, horizontal red oval with a filled-in black circle inside it—the flag of the militia known as Cyklops. Even if Roan hadn't done her research into this place, she recognizes white nationalist art design when she sees it.

The rest of the property has a scattering of outbuildings whose purpose she does not know and can only guess at. One large building looks like a dormitory—Nico told her once that more people than just the James family live here—and Roan thinks she might be right, judging by the number of people wandering about outside. In the side yard of the farmhouse, there's a large, exterior eating area with tables, chairs, and a large, wooden overhang decorated with vines and string lighting, all surrounded by mosquito torches. Across the property there are stables and one of those little circular fenced-in areas with the big spinning thing in the middle you use to train horses. (She really thinks she should have studied more about ranches in general and not just about Columbia itself before she came.) She sees an area that looks like an outdoor theater, with a stage and a backdrop and stadium seating, and finally a silo standing next to a large, brown barn that's guarded by two more of the cowboys, automatic rifles dangling lazily from their arms. They're in conversation with a nun who looks strangely out of time, buttoned up in a robe that reminds Roan of something from the days of the Inquisition. A river snakes through the landscape, the sunlight glinting off its surface like scales.

These people have all this, and Roan had to go to the bowling alley, pickpocketing drunk dads on their visitation weekends, just so she could make rent at her studio apartment this month,.

God bless America.

The cowboys lead the crowd down into the valley, passing the occasional farmhand doing chores, and each time they do, Roan looks at their faces, searching for Andrew Garrett. She doesn't find him, not before the cowboys lead the group to that exterior stage and tell them to fill up the seats. The quiet masses obey, and Roan moves quickly, selecting one of the seats at the top and the back so that she can look out over the other heads for her quarry, and so that she will not easily be looked at herself.

Everyone settles down as a barefoot brunette in a floral sundress walks onstage, but Roan's silence is different because she finally sees *him*. She knows she'll recognize that face anywhere, has it burned into her mind after everything it put her through. Andrew Garrett is standing just offstage, having come over to escort the brunette up. He's dressed just like all the other men in big work boots and dirt-stained jeans. There is a pair of gloves in his back pocket and his Henley is unbuttoned, sleeves rolled up. Like the other men, he wears a gun belt and has his thumbs looped into the front like he's an old-fashioned gunslinger, and the way he stands there, as if he doesn't have a care in the world, as if he has no idea what he's done, makes Roan hate everything about him even more.

You killed her, she thinks, struggling to maintain her composure, knowing she has to. For just a little longer.

The woman on the stage starts speaking, but Roan doesn't hear her. She is laser-focused on the man she came here to kill and how she's going to kill him, the devil on her shoulder having long ago smothered the angel's words.

MOTHER HARROW

To the people of Columbia, the woman watching the newcomers from the farmhouse window is known as Mother Harrow, even though she has no children. Though that's not for lack of trying. Harrow James has her husband's seed inside her even now as she stands there watching the initiates roll by in the direction of the church. She can feel it dried on the insides of her thighs, and shivers at the sensation.

You'll endure it, she tells herself. *Suffering builds strength.*

The Jameses tell their followers at Columbia that sex is purely for procreation, that to enjoy it is a sin, but Harrow knows Paxton doesn't really believe that, not when she sees the pleasure he very clearly gets from taking her in a myriad of creative ways. He wouldn't put his cock in her mouth or her ass if he were only interested in having children. He wouldn't have a steamer trunk filled with all manner of sex toys at the foot of their bed—gags and whips, ropes and handcuffs—if he were only interested in procreation. These are all devices Paxton himself has called sinful when outside of their bedroom, and yet he uses them all on her for his own ends. Paxton has always been one to *fuck*, rarely to *make love*, and yet lately he's become even more forceful, telling her what to do with his hands instead of his words. Just that afternoon, he'd wandered in while she was getting ready for service, and she'd forced herself to open up for him.

No, no, she tells herself, *not forced. It's your wifely duty.* Paxton seemed to have forgotten entirely about the devilish temptations of the flesh, about how Eve herself was tempted into lust by the Serpent, spawning some of the races of man.

Because he's so focused on himself, Harrow finds her own pleasures during her time with Paxton, lost not in him but the intricacies of her own mind, her own steadily growing fantasies. She lets herself focus on the individual parts of him, not who they're attached to, with Paxton himself blurring until he disappears entirely, replaced by a nebulous, star-speckled shadow, a figure of infinite possibility. Harrow doesn't know what that shadow is yet, but she knows it isn't her husband. And that means it can be *anything*. Sometimes, it's a trucker who picks up the lost, hitchhiking Harrow in the middle of the night, who takes her from behind when she offers the only payment she can: warm flesh. In her darker thoughts, it's a theoretical cousin, an inexperienced lover she spreads herself for, as they're forced to stay quiet lest they wake up those sleeping next door.

And in the darkest fantasy she's ever had, the shadow that envelopes her takes the form of the miracle that's in the barn, that nebulous, oily, ever-shifting shape.

The angel.

No, Harrow tells herself whenever those fantasies come upon her, blinking, shaking her head, as if she can dislodge the thoughts from her mind. The barn isn't somewhere she must go. At least not alone. *No one* is supposed to go to the barn alone, not even Paxton. The miracles are great, they are just, but they are also dangerous, she reminds herself.

"I don't like it," Paxton says, not really paying attention to the fact that she's not paying attention. "Lettin' these people in to see we're no Jonestown, sure, but those internet reporters?" He scoffs. "Not even from a newspaper. Not even a real TV station."

"It'll be worth it," Harrow says flatly. Paxton ignores her.

Paxton never notices when Harrow tunes out like that, becomes lost in her own head in the middle of their carnal activities or otherwise. Or if he does, he never says anything. He just keeps thrusting as he did moments ago, pumping harder, seemingly knowing he'd finish quickly because he didn't even bother taking his shirt off, just pulling his pants down around his knees. He rolled off of her, and Harrow found herself yet again playing the dutiful wife, tilting her hips and pulling her knees up to her breasts to keep his seed from spilling. At least until Paxton left the room, and then she flopped down like a starfish, relaxing her muscles.

They've yet to conceive a child. For the longest time, Harrow thought it might've been her fault, that she might be barren, unable to give Paxton a son, an heir to Columbia, to the Brotherhood of the Black Cross, to the miracle in the barn, to everything they are destined to become.

But none of his mistresses are pregnant either.

None of them talk about it.

But women don't need to talk about things to know them.

Harrow heads to her bathroom to start her getting ready routine all over again now that she's been interrupted. She checks herself in the mirror before getting in the shower, regretting it as she often does. She is the classical image of beauty, everything she's been told a woman should be, with long, dark hair that falls all the way to her waist, covering her large breasts like Lady Godiva, high cheekbones, a slender neck. She's not big enough to be considered *fat*, and yet she has wide, child-bearing hips. The way she describes her own body, as something to be seen for someone else's pleasure, sends splinters through her mind. But she doesn't know why that last phrase in particular sets her off so much: *child-bearing hips*. Something about it feels wrong in a way she knows that she knows but doesn't know if she can actually admit.

She shakes it off and bathes and dresses for the day, trying to shake all those devilish thoughts from her mind. She puts on her thick-framed glasses, an enormous pair that look like they're from the eighties and make her look bookish and unassuming. She picks a pretty floral sundress and parts her hair in the center, brushes it to flow loose over her shoulders, and slips her feet into sandals. Paxton had decided the outfit for her yesterday. Harrow pretended her opinion was heard.

Columbia is different from the typical religious retreat. From the moment Paxton first set up their church, he knew that despite the fact that he was its leader, he didn't want to be the church's voice. He was never a man to stand before a crowd and talk, at least not any more than he needed to. He was the kind of man who let his actions speak for him. But *someone* needed to speak, and who better than Harrow, the person closest to him? Men, Paxton said, are easily swayed by the temptations of power. Which is why he wanted to stand *among* his people, not above them. Senators and congressmen and judges and, hell, maybe even the president soon enough, sit in their positions for life, becoming soft and gelatinous, bending to the whims of whichever suppliant offers them the most. The NRA, Big Pharma, Silicon Valley. Even priests move from parish to parish with the illusion of impermanence, when all that really changes is their surroundings in which they commit their abuses.

Women, Paxton says, make the better preachers. They're naturally sweeter. People are more inclined to listen to them. When they talk in front of a crowd, they *want* to be heard, whereas every man he's seen, preacher or politician, *needs* to be heard.But if a woman is speaking, their husbands can stand behind them with a hand on their shoulder. Not just as watchmen to check their power, but as voices who can speak through their wives if they really need to, who can be heard without the preconceived notions that come with those senators and congressmen and judges and presidents.

Harrow wonders, as she steps out onto the front porch, what she's going to say today, to this brand new, and much larger than usual crowd they've brought into their community to help dispel the rumors of a dangerous cult. She looks out over the property, over their land, and sees her husband's world, her world, and all the people that fill it. She sees the property of Columbia, the town of Parthas in the distance, sees their fields, their church, and the cattle grazing in the distance.

The barn.

Harrow averts her eyes, as if she's just seen something indecent, and an unfamiliar sensation tickles at her. A warmth just below her belly. Like something she should've felt by Paxton's touch last night. She's suddenly wet, and it's the thought of the angel that lives in the barn that brings her there.

Harrow takes a deep breath and looks down to a rustling at her feet, and sees a small, shimmering something vanish into the grass at the side of the drive. It slithers away, and after her shock abates, she prays it takes all her dark thoughts with it.

WHISPER IN THE GARDEN

Roan only casually listens to the woman at the podium who introduces herself as Mother Harrow, as she says whatever it is she has to say. Roan tries to make it look like she isn't more interested in Andrew Garrett, who stands off to the side of the stage, but no one is paying attention to who Roan is looking at. They're clinging to Mother Harrow's every word. But whatever proselytizing she's doing largely bypasses Roan, goes in one ear and out the other. She catches the occasional *sinner* or *wicked* or *protect the children*. Something about an angel. Roan is more focused on remembering Nico, remembering the vague stories she'd tell about *the guy*, always *the guy*, never with a name, even when things between them were good. *The guy* wasn't in the picture anymore. *The guy* was a piece of shit who refused to let Nico stop at his dick in her mouth. *The guy* was a worthless motherfucker who didn't wanna stick around after he discovered the result of what he'd forced her into. Always these vagaries Nico never wanted to fully disclose, even though Roan could read between the lines. *The guy* put something inside her, a time bomb that ended up killing her.

Roan tells herself to breathe, that whatever is going to happen, it isn't going to happen here and now while this preacher is speaking. She forces herself to turn away from Garrett, at the very least to try and smother the rage she feels at being in his presence, and almost by accident tunes in to Mother Harrow's speech. After hearing everything Nico told her about this place, Roan had been expecting something much more megachurchy, something with spotlights and fireworks and huge speakers and a Christian rock band. And while Columbia is clearly flush, that isn't the vibe Roan gets from Harrow.

"Suffering," she tells the crowd, her voice amplified by a small microphone and only a pair of speakers, "is good for the soul."

Roan immediately tunes out again. She's heard this a million times before. Not just from churches, but everywhere she's gone. Different versions of the same ethos espoused by jobs, bosses, friends, lovers, people so conditioned by late-stage capitalism and not-quickly-rising-so-much-as-being-already-here religious nationalism that they don't even realize how deep the brain worms have burrowed. Churches and priests describing the suffering of the saints for the redemption of humanity. Politicians who would never in their lives meet her telling emotionless microphones and video cameras about the nobility of poverty, of a hard day's work. Jeremy Garner in the eighth grade, about to take her virginity, telling her it's gotta hurt before it feels good, and that he better not tell anyone else because two boys weren't supposed to do what they were doing.

Roan manages to latch onto a part of Harrow's sermon again, a bit that punches through: "But here in Columbia, we have something special, something no one and nowhere else has. Thanks to our angel, we have *miracles*."

Roan has heard this before. Not from Nico—she left before any of this started—but from the research she'd done before she came. The little town of Parthas had quite the history, from its start as a railroad town, the home of a famous brothel, the site of many an Old West duel, to the tornado that destroyed much of the town in the nineties, and its slow rebuild into the homebase of the Brotherhood of the Black Cross militia group. And most recently, Columbia, the self-named, privately-owned property of the James family, the sight of alleged miracles—the definition of *miracles*, of course, being entirely arbitrary. Roan's research drew up the first things people thought of when religious miracles came to mind: Marion apparitions, weeping statues, and some miraculous healing. There were a couple that at least had a little more flair, were a little more Old Testament—the river turning to blood, a rain of fish, angelic lights in the sky that were supposedly witnessed by dozens.

And then Roan read an article where an anonymous source claimed these miracles were the result of an *entity*.

But of course, this alleged entity had never been produced for any of the reports or articles. Preaching before the crowd, Harrow claims they were able to figure out the angel gave them miracles in return for offerings, but they were never able to figure out what offerings it actually wanted, and so the entirety of their communication was a guessing game. As far as excuses go, Roan thinks it's a decent one. Angels probably don't speak English.

Most of what she read in her research painted Columbia as a Jonestown in the making—snake handling, demagogues, a jingoistic mini-state where its inhabitants could complain freely about immigrants and Blacks and queers because this was America and they had a right to free speech, dammit. But the articles stopped coming when the bodies didn't start piling up. Hatred is barely news anymore unless there are bodies.

Harrow preaches propagandized versions of all the events Roan has read about, claiming some type of being is responsible for the miracles, reiterating each one Roan read about and more. She explains how they discovered the entity in the plains surrounding their home while on a horseback ride with her husband, about its ability to alter the world, and the greenery and the miracles. At a certain point, Roan tunes out.

The sermon ends after at least a couple hours—Roan has lost track of time, but the sun has moved a long way across the sky—after

Harrow claims people across the nation, across the world, will soon see. She tells them that in just a few days, a television crew will arrive, Columbia's miracles to be broadcast to the nation (soon, soon, always *soon*, never *now* with these kinds of people).

The crowd dissipates, guided by the cowboys, the Pioneers, Harrow called them, the Blackshirts of the Brotherhood of the Black Cross, leading the newcomers away from the pulpit and across the property in the direction of the farmhouse. One of the Pioneers on horseback is telling the gathered crowd all about Columbia, about the property and its history, but Roan isn't paying attention and is instead thinking about all the ways she's familiar with cult programming, with relationships with power imbalances. She's sure that woman, Harrow, was chosen specifically. She's sure there is a level of groupthink behind her appearance, behind her hair, her makeup, that specific sundress. Someone wanted her out on that stage looking like a tradwife, like a beautiful, Edenic image of a woman, someone who could offer anyone anything, someone that no one could find any real offense in, unlike so many of the male demagogues in politics now, who claimed they were right just because they were the loudest.

Roan thinks of the snakes who twitch those little yellow, wormlike ends of their tails to lure prey. Is Harrow complicit in this place, or is she another victim, even if she doesn't know it? She's the little yellow tail for sure, but is she the one wriggling, or is she being moved by the rest of the snake?

Roan watches for the inevitable love bombing. It's not the same as the honeymoon phase, the part of a normal relationship where two people meet and become infatuated. No, in a place like this, the love comes first, and it comes in tidal waves. It comes so hard and so fast you're never ready for it. And just as quickly, it gets taken away, becomes conditional, and by then it's too late, and you'll do anything to get that love back.

The Pioneers lead the new group of initiates into the farmhouse's side yard, to that enormous eating area where a feast has been laid out. Another trap. Roan is sure plenty of these people are hungry, if not outright starving (they'd been listening to Harrow preach all afternoon), and she can't think of a quicker way to secure someone's allegiance than feeding them.

She'd be lying if she said she didn't feel that pull at least a little bit, a hook behind her heart, that want to belong here, anywhere. But she knows they'd never accept her. Not a man who's pretending to be a woman, they'd call her. Not a monster, they'd say. Not a pedophile. So bigoted they can't even understand the differences between the things they hate. And yet even with these things they'd call her, it's easy to see how Nico could have become so drawn into this.

But Roan's desire for revenge is stronger than her desire for belonging because her belonging is gone, dead, gave its last gasp on a bloody hospital bed with only Roan by her side, because Nico's parents could not forgive unwed motherhood, let alone queerness. Roan remembers what she came here for and holds on to it.

While the new initiates take their seats around the many long tables, Roan scans the crowd for Andrew Garrett. She sees him appear sporadically, watching him as the new initiates eat their first meal in Columbia. After it's finished, people begin to get up, move around, and talk amongst one another. As the sun begins to set, the Pioneers light the mosquito torches and the bonfires, and the exterior lights on the buildings begin to blink on. Roan is about to get up too, to begin her search for the lost specter of Garrett, when the empty seat next to her is suddenly occupied.

Harrow James sits down next to her.

"Hello," she says, catching Roan by surprise. "You're new here. You don't look like our... usual newcomers. What brings you to Columbia?"

A sudden panic hits Roan. Besides the thought that she might be found out, that she might be clocked, might be discovered and summarily executed (a fear she doesn't know is paranoia or possibility), she hasn't thought far enough ahead to consider she might have to make anything beyond small talk. She has always been so laser-focused on her goal she never thought she'd have to explain herself, her backstory, to anyone. Let alone the leader of this retreat. She decides to remain vague.

"There was a death in the family. I'm just..." She cringes, trails off, hopes it's enough, remembers the sporadic encounters she's had with overly-religious people in the past, those who thought she needed some sort of intervention and who wanted to press their lifestyle in on her while complaining about other peoples' lifestyle being forced down their own throats. She thinks about a woman who asked her, when she worked at the post office, to pray over the delivery of her package, that it made it to its destination safely, and who became surly and then eventually called her a bitch when Roan simply said it made her uncomfortable. And an old man who tipped Roan what appeared to be a hundred dollar bill for serving him and his post-church brunch, but when she turned it over discovered it was fake, printed with a message about how she needed to be Saved—capital S—and the instructions on how to do so by accepting Jesus Christ as her lord and savior. She expects something similar from Harrow, but she doesn't get it.

"Well, you've come to the right place," Harrow says, and that's all she says. Roan sits there, waiting for her to say more, to maybe ask about this death, to reassure Roan that the dead person, whomever they may be, is waiting in Heaven—capital H—for her. So long as she herself is saved, of course. But, no, Harrow says nothing and seems content to sit with Roan in silence. That makes Roan almost as uncomfortable, and she suddenly finds the need to fill the space. She recognizes the tactic from many a therapy session.

"So, where's the thing?" she asks, picking the first topic of conversation her brain can find. She speaks, of course, of this alleged *entity*.

"In the barn," Harrow says, surprisingly forthcoming. She gestures with her chin, and Roan follows, looking down the hill to the big, red building. A group of those Pioneers are still standing outside guarding it.

"Are you serious?" she asks, looking back.

Harrow nods.

"Can I go see it?" She thinks to call the woman's bluff. If it's really down there, there's no harm in just looking at it, right? Roan wonders what the excuse will be when the door opens and nothing's there.

"No," Harrow says. "It's not for everyone."

Roan wonders if there's a sort of payment plan. Put up to the highest tier, and you can go into the barn and see some big, elaborate puppetry, smoke and mirrors disguised as a fallen angel, or whatever the thing is supposed to be. Part of her remembers there was an old Roman emperor who did something like that.

"But we'll show the world in time," Harrow says. "We have a television crew coming here to show everyone our gift."

"That'll show 'em," Roan says, not really wanting to push the conversation any further, not wanting to engage any more than she has to with this woman, not wanting to invite her scrutiny. Roan's sure whatever they do to trans people here, it's nothing good. She looks around for Andrew Garrett, trying to get Harrow to take the hint, but she doesn't and remains seated.

After a moment, a man in a cowboy hat comes over. He bends down next to Harrow and whispers something in her ear. Roan aims to ignore the interaction, but when she sees the man touch Harrow, she suddenly knows she can't. Something takes her over, compels her to look back, to see the man's hand not just rest on her shoulder but see his fingers squeeze. It's a slight motion, something someone might never notice the truth of if they weren't looking for it, if they weren't used to the small ways in which men exerted their power over women. But Roan knows this language. She recognizes its subtleties and dialects. She watches the two of them talk out of the corner of her eye, watches as the man's hand changes on Harrow's shoulder, letting go with his right and gently grabbing the back of her neck with his left as their talk became more hushed. She sees Harrow's eyes widen, sees her grip the armrests of her chair, her toes curl in her sandals like Roan's do on the rare occasion she can afford to go to the dentist.

"Yes, honey," Harrow says, not looking at the man as he whispers in her ear, but into the middle distance, and when he releases her, she still doesn't unclench until he's far away.

"Good," is all the man says as he turns and walks away. He doesn't even acknowledge Roan.

The devil on Roan's shoulder hijacks her brain.

"Who was that?" she asks. The devil slams the gas pedal with its spiked heels, turning the music up and lowering the windows, sticking the pitchfork out into the air. She feels a sudden desire for revenge against this man. Not the death she seeks for Andrew Garrett—at least not yet—but a small revenge. Like when a drunk girl at a pool hall had got to talking to her, confessed she knew her boyfriend was cheating, but hadn't yet confronted him about it. Roan convinced him to upper deck the toilet in his apartment and leave a note on the mirror.

"My husband," Harrow says. She suddenly seems aware of how tense she is and that this is not how a woman is supposed to act in the presence of her husband. She unclenches, uncrossing and recrossing her legs, smoothing her dress. She tries and fails to hide letting out a deep breath.

"Husband," Roan says, watching the man finally disappear through the crowd. "He's not the leader here?"

"Oh, he is," Harrow says. "He's just not the face. People have an easier time trusting a woman."

Wonder why that is, Roan thinks.

"Especially," Harrow continues, "in a climate such as this." She gestures to the fields, indicating Columbia.

"Yeah, Jones and Koresh really didn't do anybody any favors." She could've thought of more contemporary comparisons, but she really doesn't want to get kicked out.

Harrow gives her a look, something inscrutable, but again, she doesn't say anything. Roan can't get a bead on this woman.

"Trust is hard for anybody, though," Roan says, trying to lead her on. An idea is forming in her head, and she wonders if she can get it out. She just has to find a way to speak Harrow's language. "Goes all the way back to the beginning. I mean the *beginning* beginning."

"You mean Eve?" Harrow asks.

Hook.

Harrow says, "I'm surprised. You don't seem very religious."

"I went to Sunday school." Sometimes. The idea is hatching inside Roan's head, taking shape even as it's coming out of her. The devil on her shoulder is screaming down the highway, blasting backmasked Santanic jams.

"Although it wasn't really Eve's fault," Harrow says. "The Devil very nearly deceived Jesus himself. We can all fall prey to temptation."

Roan wonders what sorts of things tempt Harrow, and that curiosity begins to lead her down a road she hasn't expected.

"Did Adam really have another wife?" Roan asks. "Before Eve, I mean. I remember hearing that somewhere."

Harrow nods. *Line.* "Depending on who you ask. Some say it was Lilith, but she was exiled from the Garden."

"For what?" Roan asks. But she knows.

"Disobedience," is all Harrow says. *Sinker.* It's all she needs to say. Roan hasn't planted the seed. It was already there. All she did was give it some water and sunlight.

TILL DEATH DO US PART

"Do you think you're gonna shit when you pop this lil bean out?" Roan asked, rubbing Nico's swollen belly as they lay in bed, sunlight streaming through the apartment's windows.

"Absolutely," Nico said. She reached out and took Roan's face in her hand. "And you're gonna have to watch it all."

"Will they let me?" she asked. "Will they let me be there?" She didn't know what the rules were anymore. They were not legally bound in any way. Two unmarried people. Unmarried women. One of them not a real woman at all, depending on who you asked. The fear, the anxiety, was only there for a moment before Roan realized it didn't matter. She hadn't ever followed the rules and wouldn't start now. Just let them try to keep her out. She knew she'd be there, knew she'd watch. Watch Nico shit herself or watch the child breach or crown or whatever the hell it was called. Watch every beautiful, disgusting moment. She'd see anything, no matter how horrible it sounded, if it was with Nico.

THE LURE

Roan wonders if this is how a lioness feels during the hunt, this sense of power. Her prey lingers on the outside edges of the crowd with the other Pioneers, and when Roan looks at him, she sees him already eyeing at her and thinks this might be even easier than she thought. She doesn't even need to try to get his attention. To get any of their attention, really. All Roan has to do is *exist* in this space in order to gather attention. She's hyperaware of the eyes that are on her because she's a woman, and the eyes that are on her because she is different from all the others.

Despite how she's long ago settled that Andrew Garrett's death is what has to happen, Roan can still feel her angel and her demon duking it out. It feels like they entered her brain through her ears, just like in the cartoons, and are throwing down inside her skull. She silences the angel as she wanders through the crowd, making small chitchat with the other initiates and the occasional Pioneer, smart enough not to go straight for Garrett, not to give anything away, to make it too easy.

No, she makes him come to her. Makes it seem like it's his idea. Like he's in control. She gives him the occasional glance as she mingles, the half-smile that any man would take as an instant invitation, regardless of actual intent. As the sun sets, she casually takes off her outer shirt and wraps it around her waist, exposing her bare, tattooed arms, the low cut of her tank top. She doesn't have to feign a sweat with the summer humidity. She pulls her purple hair up into a messy bun, glancing over at Garrett as she does. She is the snake with the wriggling tail, and he comes right over to her, looking for a meal.

"Hey, newbie," Garrett says once he finally sidles up. Does he know she's trans? Is that the point of his approach? Is he one of the men who so desperately wants to *try*, but doesn't want to be seen as gay?

"Hi." Roan plays bashful, quiet, an interior that doesn't match an exterior, but she knows Garrett is too blind to notice. Surely, his blood is somewhere else besides his brain.

"Name's Andrew," he says, offering his hand.

She thinks about lying, about making up a fake name, spinning an identity from whole cloth, but by this time tomorrow, it won't matter what he knows, because he won't know anything. His skull will be an empty hollow.

"Roan," she says, holding out her own hand daintily, uncharac- teristically, and by the way Garrett takes her hand in both of his, she knows she has him in her thrall.

THE NAME

"This baby's gonna have one of those basic white girl names, isn't it? Like Aiden or Nevaeh." Roan placed the tip of her finger against Nico's belly, swirling spiral patterns across her skin.

"I haven't thought of a name yet," Nico said, rubbing her stomach, her own hand following Roan's, catching up to it, intertwining their fingers. Roan knew the dad wouldn't have any say in it. She didn't know who the dad was then, only that he was gone. It didn't matter who the dad was then, because he was gone. "Would you want to help me pick one?"

"Me?"

"Yes, you," Nico said. "You're the one who'll be here for it." And then, asking for affirmation, "Won't you?"

Roan took Nico's face in her hands.

"Of course, I will."

And then her lips in hers.

THE BODY AND THE BLOOD

Roan has harmed, but she has never killed anyone before. She's harmed plenty of people, plenty of *men*, specifically, because they meant to her harm first. Not even *tried* but *meant to*. An absolute intention. She didn't even give them the chance. A guy in a hoodie who'd followed her from the bar because she ignored his supposed "compliment." He'd ended up with a face full of pepper spray and a handful of broken fingers. A man only a few years ago who grew angry with her when she withdrew conditional consent when he choked her. She'd felt one of his balls pop in her fist. A woman who clocked her in the woman's bathroom of an airport. Roan had kicked her in the shin with steel-toed boots.

Which is not to say Andrew Garrett doesn't mean her harm or won't attempt to harm her. Just because he wants something from her—something, for all he suspects, she fully intends to give him—doesn't mean he still won't hurt her to get it.

It's remarkably easy to get him interested in her, remarkably easy to get him alone, to get him tipsy, though she doesn't think she needs to. He's blinded by something other than liquor, by the lack of blood in his brain. Roan tells him a walk might be nice, down by the river, watching the sun set where no one can see them. They make conversation, but she's only halfway aware of it, focusing instead on her body and on Garrett's relation to it. He gives her a small touch here, a little look there.

You deserve this, what's about to happen, she thinks as they crest a hill and come down to the edge of the river. *You pressured her into sex, you fucking* raped *her, and that killed her.* She thinks about finding a moment to explain this—herself, the past, everything leading up to this moment, like a movie villain monologue—but he doesn't deserve it.

He took Nico from her.

He deserves nothing.

"You can still," she purrs, looking at him as they stand there on the bank of the river, "fool around a little bit?" She bites her lip, lifts her right foot up to perch on her toes. She looks at him doe eyed. She hates herself for it.

"Yeah," Garrett smirks. "We're not priests."

And without waiting, Roan kisses him. She hates herself for it, hates the feel of his greedy hands on her, even though these are the same hands that touched Nico, and this is probably the closest she'll ever be to her again. His hands grope her back, her ass, fingers slipping in under the waist of her jeans, and then he unexpectedly pulls away.

"Are you..." he asks, not finishing the sentence, letting it hang because he can't finish it, can't say the words, and needs her to.

"Am I what?" she asks, playing at being a plaything, but she knows exactly what he wants to say as he looks over her muscles, her tattoos, her throat. *Are you a man? Are you a tranny? What are you working with? Do you have a pussy, or do I have to fuck you in the ass?*

Without another word, Roan squats before him to get those hands away from her, to get those questions out of his head, not going all the way down to her knees, but squatting because she knows she'll need to move fast with what's about to happen. As Garrett fumbles with his belt, the questions he wanted to ask completely forgotten, she thinks of all the men and women and everyone in between she's pleasured before, and the ways in which they reacted to the offering of her liminal body. If she were to generalize, she'd stick to the Gs: the women were always grateful, while the men were always greedy.

Garrett continues the trend, ripping his fly open, his gun belt weighing his pants down, pulling them off his hips for him. He holds his hands awkwardly at his sides, boxers tented out, silently telling Roan to do it, as if giving her the honor. She puts her hands on his hips and yanks his boxers down, his dick popping free, pre-cum already oozing out of the end. She tries to look at it and not at the gun that is oh-so-very-close.

She works her tongue in her mouth, welling up spit, thinking about how Nico did this to him, about how it was all she wanted to do, but he wouldn't stop, how he fucked her to a death that wouldn't reach her for another nine months. Roan thinks about Nico lying on her back, Garrett thrusting into her, and she tries to use the familiar image of Nico's flushed skin as a lifeline to take her away, for just as long as she needs to, but then Garrett's hands are on the back of her head, pushing her towards him, and he's in her mouth before she's ready, thrusting past lips and teeth. *She gave you the gift of her body, but only so much. And when that wasn't enough for you, you killed her.* Roan doesn't choke on his cock because she knows how not to, and because Garrett simply isn't big enough, though she's sure plenty of women have told him he is. She can feel him relax. His hands loosen their grip on her hair, leaning backwards as she moves her mouth along him, swirls her tongue around him, working herself into a rhythm she knows will distract him, not finish him.

Nico, she thinks, *was it hard and red like this when you were with him, or was it softer, sweeter? Did you* need *it, or did you* want *it? Did you kneel here before him, supplicant like a worshiper?* Roan wonders as she lifts her left hand to Garrett's cock. She lets it go on a bit longer than she knows she has to, or probably even should, because in some fucked-up way it makes her just a little bit closer to Nico, the two of them sharing one last thing before the world changes in an even harsher way than it has with her death.

Roan yanks the revolver from its holster on the ground and Garrett is too busy to notice, his buttocks and hips and abs tensing as he's about to come already. His dick is still in her mouth as she pulls the hammer back with her right hand, as she pushes him suddenly away with her left, standing up, bringing the barrel to bear.

It doesn't happen in slow-motion like it does in movies, but in a sort of vacuum. Like everything in the world has ceased to exist except Roan, Garrett, and the gun. Even the landscape has evaporated, turning to nothing, leaving them in an endless, dark void. Just as the killing doesn't happen in slow-motion, the gunshot doesn't tear apart the world like Roan is expecting. It's loud, yes, and she certainly feels it buck in her hand, but maybe it's the rush of blood in her ears, maybe it's the wide-open plain that lets the sound dissipate, or maybe it's the fact that ever since she saw Nico laid out on a slab she's been screaming inside her own head, louder than any gunshot, louder than any sound that's ever existed.

The first bullet takes Garrett in the gut, folds him in half, and Roan can see it blast out of his back, a spray of blood tainting the river behind him. She even sees the splash of the bullet hitting the water.

He looks up just in time for the second shot to take half his face off.

The left side of Andrew Garrett's face evaporates, and he leans back, arms windmilling as he attempts to save himself from falling, but then Roan is moving. The gun is gone somewhere in the river because it's too impersonal, a cold and metal and distant thing. She needs to finish this not with the impersonality of a bullet, but the rage that only bare hands can muster. She throws herself at him, tackling him, shoving him down into the river, both of them submerging, and she can already feel that he's nothing in her grasp, that all his resistance is gone. Roan surfaces, hands finding Garrett's shoulders, keeping him under the water. She looks down and sees him beneath her, his face a ruin. He's trying to close his mouth, but he has no lips beyond his left incisor, and Roan can see the blood and air rushing out from between his cracked and missing teeth, the water rushing in. He tries to break free, but Roan's justice is inevitable. She wants this more than him.

He merely wants to live, while she needs him to die.

PART 2:

THE SCARLET COLORED BEAST

TOO MUCH EVIL

"When I was a little girl, I had this Aunt Cathy," Nico once told her. They'd been sitting together on the couch, Nico balancing a plate of pizza on her belly, Roan by her side. There was some black and white horror movie on television, but Roan didn't think she even knew what it was. She'd popped in the nearest DVD from an old bargain bin collection in order to get away from the endless stream of terrible news that flashed across the TV. There was too much evil in the world, and the stream of it was unrelenting, demagogues standing before rallied crowds, living skeletons in judge's robes handing down rulings that made Roan and Nico steadily more and more afraid. It made them wonder if Roan was going to be able to continue her treatments, or, God forbid, what they would do if anything happened to the baby. The images pushed parasites into their heads, spiked their adrenaline, and they had to get away from it, go back to simpler times, when all people had to worry about was whether or not they'd make it away from the zombie apocalypse or the alien invasion or the ghouls or whatever was happening.

And, really, it didn't matter what the movie was. It was an excuse for them to get scared and huddle closer to one another. A shield that kept the outside world at bay, made sure only the two of them existed. Just for a moment. Just for ninety minutes.

"Aunt Cathy was one of those relatives you only ever saw at holidays, weddings, or funerals," Nico continued. "Anyway, this was one of those few times a year I saw her. At someone's baptism. I didn't even know what a baptism was at that point. I was just a little kid. I remember sitting there in my floral dress, bored with the church music and the heat and the chalky smell of old people. And Aunt Cathy, leaning over from the pew behind me, told me that when every baby is born, they would get a baptism if they weren't a dirty heathen, and that meant putting a baby in the water and hoping they wouldn't get weighed down by too much innate evil."

"Jesus Christ!" Roan gasped. She didn't need to look away from the movie; she was already gazing up at Nico. She knew it was a strange thought, considering their relationship, but she wondered if this was how it felt to be a baby and look up at your mother, at someone who might as well have been a deity. There were different kinds of love, different words that encapsulated what it meant to love, and Roan knows she felt and continues to feel more than just one kind of love for Nico.

"Are you gonna get her baptized?" she asked then, lying out over the couch, her head on Nico's shoulder. She saw something pass through her then, a flicker of a thing, there and then gone. A fear she had never seen on Nico's face before, and would only ever see once, the last time she ever saw that face. A fear of something greater, of something cosmic and eternal that suddenly swelled up out of nowhere. A fear she didn't know she had.

PRIDE

Too much evil. Roan thinks about Nico's Aunt Cathy as she lets go of Garrett's body, as he refuses to come back to the surface. Too much evil in him, that was for sure.

She thought it would feel different. Not just the killing itself, but revenge. *Justice.* Because that's what this is. She didn't think she'd hear cinematic music descending from the heavens or anything like that, but she thought she'd feel... something. She looks down at the red ruin of Garrett's face just under the water and thinks, *huh*. There's nothing. No feeling at all.

This isn't good. She doesn't think that about the murder, about the potential punishment she faces in this place should she be caught (surely some medieval shit), but about herself and where she stands and the complete absence of feeling aside from the river water rushing over her thighs and the wind in her hair. It's been too long, she knows, too long since she's activated that mental defense mechanism, too long since she's allowed herself to feel anything at all. Is the door back to feelings closed permanently now? Has Roan shut it off for good? Is there a way to get emotions back if you've burned them out of you?

There should be something, she thinks, even as she strips the gun belt from the waist of his pants (which are bunched around his knees), as she bends down into the river to pick up the revolver. She wades out of the river and to the shore, watching over her shoulder as Garrett's body catches on a rock, still under, bobbing gently as the river pulls at it. She watches the corpse as she dries herself as best she can on

Garrett's discarded jacket and shirt and then throws the gun belt over her shoulder like a damsel in an old Western.

There's nothing but an empty hole inside her.

Until...

You did so good.

Roan looks up, thinking she heard a voice, but there's no one. Just her and the river. Just her and the night.

And yet.

You did so good, *baby.*

The words strike at the core of her, just as they did the first time Nico ever said them to her. Because that's whose voice it is, of course. Nico's. Roan wants to pretend it isn't, but there's no denying it. It floats there on the wind, across the surface of the river, tickling her earlobe just like Nico's lips used to.

She wants to say it, but doesn't want to talk to the air, to the nothing. Because Nico isn't there, is only in Roan's head. And yet she can't stop herself.

"Are you proud of me?"

I'm so goddamn proud of you, the Roan-projected Nico says, and a little fire finally lights up in Roan's chest.

Garrett is dead.

It's over. Time to leave.

FIG LEAVES

Paxton James lifts his head at the sound through their open window, and Harrow registers it a moment later. It's two gunshots, in quick succession, and from a pistol, considering the tiny *pop* of the echo. Hearing gunshots on their property isn't exactly a rare occurrence—hell, they have a shooting range—but it is something to be aware of.

Harrow watches as Paxton slides out of bed, and as he does, she hangs onto the sheets, keeping herself covered from the chest down. Just a little bit of her leg hangs out from under the sheet, and she imagines she must look like a woman on the cover of a paperback romance novel. She suddenly wonders why she feels the need to cover herself in front of her husband, someone she's made love to hundreds of times before, someone she shares her entire life with. Why does she always feel embarrassed to be seen this way by him?

You know, says a little voice in her head, the same one that tempted her to conjure those fantasies about the thing in the barn. *You know why. Say it.* But she cannot.

Paxton, as usual, seems to feel no such shame. He strides naked out of bed, over to the window, seemingly unconcerned anyone below will glimpse his nudity. He's strong, chiseled, everything a woman is supposed to ever want in a man. Physically, anyway. So why does Harrow feel such shame at the sight of him, at the knowledge of the things he's done to her, was just doing to her? And how is it fair that he seems to feel what she does not? Paxton walks away from the bed, still sweating and panting, still covered in the fluids of their lovemaking, his damp, softened cock hanging free. Utterly unconcerned. And yet Harrow covers herself with the sheet as Eve did with leaves, doesn't want to look at what's surely become the smeary mess of her pelvis.

"Is everything all right?" Harrow asks as Paxton stands before the open window, looking out over the fields. She knows it isn't the shot itself that disturbs him but the fact that it's from a pistol. It's not someone hunting. It can't be target practice, not with the sun going low. It's an unknown, and he doesn't like unknowns, especially not on his property, not in his world. Paxton remains silent, doesn't answer her, and Harrow knows something else in his brain has taken over. The problem-solving part of man is now in charge.

After all, a gunshot is a far easier problem for him to solve than what just happened between them in bed.

Paxton had guided Harrow to bed in his usual quiet but stern way, pushing her in the direction of the mattress while he undressed himself, while he allowed Harrow to step out of her dress. It was all so mechanical, the romance long-since withered. Paxton only kissed her only at Harrow's insistence, and then he was on top of her, inside her, grunting and thrusting like an animal.

It was when she realized he wasn't looking at her that something seemed to take her over. Paxton looked away, focusing on a spot on the pillow next to her head, while Harrow could feel him soften inside her for no other reason than the natural struggles of an older man. He struggled to keep up, and as Harrow felt his arms quaking, she said, "Let me," and before even she knew what she was doing, she was on top. She flipped him over and straddled him, somehow all without letting him leave her, and Paxton was rock hard again, his eyes bulging at this sudden and unexpected role reversal. Harrow bucked her hips once, twice, three times, and when she reached that holy number Paxton moaned loudly and she felt her husband shudder and quake and release inside her, and they were left in the awkward aftermath of what was clearly a transgression neither of them knew how to address.

"Paxton?" Harrow asks, looking across the bedroom at him but thinking of that woman, Roan, and what she'd said to Harrow after Paxton had grabbed her shoulder after the sermon. Had she done this?

Was it her voice whispering in Harrow's ear? Was she responsible for this, or was Harrow just trying to avoid blaming herself?

"Gunshot," her husband says without looking at her. To himself, but loud enough for her to hear, he mutters "First the visitors, then the news, now this." As if it's her fault. Paxton picks up the walkie-talkie from his belt at the foot of the bed. When he ignores her and radios the rest of the Pioneers, Harrow knows they're not going to talk about what just happened. This indiscretion. Not right now. Probably not at all, knowing how Paxton handles problems. What will probably happen is that Paxton will reassert his dominance in the only ways he knows how—giving her more orders as a wife, taking her again, tomorrow night, in a position of his choosing. Claiming her. Putting her in her place. Maybe finishing on her face as a particular humiliation.

And yet Harrow cannot help but revel in the memory of the transgression.

She leans against the headboard, absentmindedly aware of Paxton calling various Pioneers over his walkie, telling them to sound off one by one, but all she can think about is the sight of him beneath her and the look of surprise on his face as she placed her hands on his chest, holding him down as he came.

And then she thinks of the woman again, Roan. The one who convinced her to do this. Well, maybe not *convinced* her, but planted the seed in her head, whether she meant to or not, and Harrow thinks she did. Just moments ago, Harrow thought her some kind of devil. Not literally, of course, but the warm whispering in her ear, the sly seductions. Now, though, after what she felt... There's something different inside Harrow. Something's hatched.

"Goddamn it, Garret, answer me!"

The blasphemy draws Harrow back to the world, to Paxton standing there half dressed, walkie raised to his lips. He releases the button, hoping for an answer but receiving nothing. He looks at Harrow. "Get up. Get dressed."

It takes her a moment to catch up, to realize why, but after a moment she knows Paxton's reassertion of dominance will not exclusively come later, but right now, in the form of action, in the form of witnessed problem-solving. Something's wrong, and he wants Harrow to see something being wrong and see him fix it. How does she know these things? How is she suddenly so aware of them? What happened to *yes, sweetheart, just a moment, husband?* Something's changing inside her. She can feel it.

And she doesn't bristle from it.

Harrow barely has time to get her dress back over her head before Paxton pulls her out of the house. He practically tosses her into the back row of his large pickup truck, in which three other Pioneers are waiting. Young, faithful men, high-and-tight haircuts, a couple visible tattoos—crosses, stars, American flags, the red eye of Cyklops, the Black Cross. True believers. The truck tires growl against the gravel as the spotlight and the top rack of lights come on, illuminating the darkness they push into.

SEE THE LIGHT

Time passes in a blur. A choppy montage. Roan wades from the river and wanders into the darkness. The night swallows her. She doesn't have her bearings, but it doesn't matter. She just walks through the dark. At some point, sunlight slowly starts encroaching on the world from behind her. She thinks about how it's over, about how she expected to feel... anything. Maybe not happiness, but perhaps at least some relief. Instead, there's still just numbness. A hole growing wider and wider. The darkness that swallowed Nico coming for her too, that tiny light sparked by Nico's voice sputtering and struggling to stay alive.

Roan thinks about how young she is, only in her thirties, and even though she parties hard and treats her body like whatever the opposite of a temple is—a football stadium men's room?—she can still expect to live a pretty long life. Is she supposed to live the rest of that life without Nico? Is she supposed to go on for another forty, fifty years in the chaos that the world is quickly becoming? Columbia was just a microcosm of what was happening all around the country. Openly-accepted fascism, white nationalism. Roan didn't know if the world was the most dangerous it'd ever been, but it was certainly the most dangerous she'd ever seen it. Certainly, for someone like her. If she were to be caught in Columbia, the same thing would happen to her that would happen to her anywhere else: she'd be branded a freak, a child predator, a danger to womanhood and America itself. Killed, whether through the legal system or otherwise. And how much more would the world change while she was around? How much worse would it get? She doesn't think she can handle doing this alone. She doesn't know if it's possible. The future is a yearning maw ready to swallow her whole, and part of her wants to let it take her so it'll all be ov er.

Roan stops in the middle of the field and looks out at the darkness all around her. Maybe this is it, she thinks. The darkness. What the rest of life is going to look like soon enough. Endless swaths of black nothing, even the stars above covered. She wants to be the kind of person who would find something meaningful in the lights that suddenly appear and the moment in which they appear, but she knows they are only headlights, only the Pioneers searching for her.

Roan wants to feel something as a huge spotlight atop the truck sweeps across the plains, but even though there's nothing but open space, nowhere for her to hide, and she'll surely be killed, she continues to feel nothing, that hole inside her swallowing everything, sputtering out that tiny light she had only a moment ago. She is startlingly aware of the things people—but especially men—can do to women before they kill them, and she knows these men would do those things to her, even though they don't consider her a woman at all. Roan is prepared to fight back, to spare herself that pain, those red indignities, and make them kill her quickly, because that's certainly their intent because of her mere existence, let alone after what she's done.

The truck comes to a stop some twenty feet away, and the passenger door pops open, Roan sees the shadow of a man step out, but another, smaller one suddenly scurries past him, stepping out around the door and into the glow of the headlights.

"Wait, stop!" the shape calls, and Roan recognizes the voice. Combined with that hourglass silhouette, Roan realizes it's the woman who was preaching earlier: Mother Harrow. She wonders if that poison is still in her ear, if Roan made one final defiance before she leaves this world. "It's you," Harrow says. The spotlight moves out of her eyes, and Roan can see four men, all armed, all standing around the truck as if it's cover, as if she's ready to start shooting at any second. Four men and Harrow, bathed in the headlights.

"It's okay," Harrow says. "We're not going to hurt you."

Roan doesn't draw the pistol, but she gestures to it hanging from her shoulder.

"You know what I did?" she says. It's not really a question.

"We found his body by the river," Harrow says.

"So, you know what I did, and you say you're not gonna hurt me?"

"No, we're not going to hurt you." Harrow shakes her head, for just a moment looking over her shoulder at the shape that must certainly be her husband. He looks like he's ready to kill, but something in Harrow's look stops him. Roan wonders what it is. If this man has ever obeyed a woman in his life. For some reason, Roan wants to hurt the man even more than she did before.

"Suffering is supposed to be good for the soul, isn't it?"

He looks like he's going to move on her, but Harrow interrupts him.

"Why did you kill Andrew?"

"Because he killed my friend," Roan says, not really surprised at her own honesty. It's just like telling Garrett her real name; it doesn't matter. It's the truth. Nothing can stop it. Nothing can undo it. "They were together. He made her have sex with him—raped her—got her pregnant and then left her before it went bad. And even when it did, he was nowhere to be found." She sees all the shadowed heads behind Harrow look at one another. Their body language doesn't change much. She wonders how much these men know about Andrew Garrett. She wonders if they know about Nico specifically. Did Garrett ever tell them her story? Was she even a chapter in his life? Even a footnote? Or just an anonymous notch in his belt?

"So, you came here for revenge," Harrow says.

"Please don't quote the Bible or tell me to turn the other cheek or some shit. It's so tiresome."

"I wasn't going to."

Roan can tell the woman's being honest. She looks at her, surprised, and decides to test her. "He fucking deserved it."

Harrow says, "Very likely he did," and again, Roan can tell she means it. Who is this woman? She feels different from the person who preached in front of the crowd only a couple of hours ago. Different even from the woman Roan spoke to. Harder. Realer. Like that was only a persona and this is the real her, unveiled by the dark.

"So..." Roan leads, "what do we do now? Are *you all* gonna turn the other cheek?"

Harrow opens her mouth to answer, but something happens. Something inexplicable. There is a light, and Roan at first thinks it is the spotlight on top of the truck turned towards her again, but it is both softer and more distant. A blue-purple light coming not from one direction but from everywhere. She looks up, and Harrow's face, the Pioneers' faces, all follow her, and she sees the source. The clouds above them have peeled away, revealing the stars. But not just the stars. Roan knows what she witnesses is not a normal, if beautiful, celestial sight. Not even an aurora borealis. What she sees isn't just a sky full of bright lights but an infinite, cosmic unveiling, the mask of the universe itself pulled back. The stars themselves brighten and shine until night turns into a beautiful lavender twilight, bathing them in cosmic colors, and that sputtering little flame inside her roars to life, swells into a conflagration, Roan can't just see, but can *feel*.

She can feel again.

She looks up into that light, and it feels like a gigantic, ethereal hand has come down and scooped whatever it is out of her that blunted her emotions, effortlessly removing it like a malignant tumor. It tears that thing out of her and throws it away, and in its place, into that void, suddenly rushes everything she's ever felt, all the beauty and pain in the world, filling her up, making her whole again.

Come to me, that voice says, the one that spoke to her in the shape of Nico. *Come.*

"It's a sign. Another miracle. The angel wants her spared."

Harrow's voice draws Roan back down to Earth, and she realizes she was actually standing on tiptoes, actually trying to rise up and reach the light. It fades slowly, but it doesn't take the feelings with it. It leaves them with Roan as the lights in the sky darken and they're left with only the natural light of the stars.

Come to me, the Nico-voice says, fading. *The barn*.

When Roan looks over at the others, she sees the woman pressing her husband's gun barrel down to the ground. "The Miracle of the Stars." She looks at Roan. "The moment we see her." She turns to the Pioneers, and they all slowly lower their weapons, all relax, except for her husband. "It's a sign, don't you see?!" Harrow looks back over her shoulder at Roan, smile wide and lighting up her face as bright as the night sky just was. It's gorgeous, Roan thinks, and as she thinks that, a spark inside her lights, a spark she immediately forces herself to stamp out of existence, to grind into the dirt. How dare she? How dare she feel something, even a small glimmer, for someone in the absence of Nico? *You should be penitent*, she tells herself. *You should be hurting*. She flagellates herself in her mind.

Harrow walks away from her husband and right up to Roan, grabbing her hands.

"You heard it, didn't you?" she asks. "The voice?"

Roan tenses, realizes she's holding Harrow's hands tighter.

"You... heard it too?"

Harrow nods.

"Come with me, please. To the barn. We're going to show you the angel."

Against what she thinks she should feel, Roan finds herself saying yes.

THE SEED

Roan expects them to blindfold her. To handcuff her. To do *something*. They don't even take her gun. Maybe it's because of the voice. She still doesn't turn her back on any of the men, expecting them to shoot her in the back of the head like a rabid dog the moment they get the chance. But they do nothing, true to Harrow's word, and even though Roan doesn't know any of these people from Adam, she senses something has changed among them. She supposes something like that was bound to happen after they just saw the stars open up, after they heard a voice from on high. Roan didn't know what it was, but surely this place interpreted it as a sign from God.

Is it really you? Roan wonders, clutching the gun tight in her fists. Could the miracles of Columbia actually be real?

They put Roan into the tiny back row of the pickup truck with Harrow, let her hold the gun in both hands, pointed straight ahead. Harrow's husband spends the whole ride turned in his seat to face her. He says nothing, just watches, unblinking, like a reptile. Roan can feel his hatred.

Andrew Garrett's waterlogged body is in the back, wrapped in a tarp. She saw it when she came around to the side, noticed the two slowly spreading bloodstains on the head and the gut. Upon seeing his body, she feels something in her chest. It's just a little bit, a spark, but it's there, the feeling of revenge, of righteousness.

"I'm sorry about your friend," Harrow says as the truck bounces through the night. "She's in a better place."

Roan says nothing. She wants to believe that but doesn't, not even with these newfound feelings. No, Nico might not be in *a better place*, but could she actually be here? Could she be close? The devil on Roan's shoulder tells her to stop believing such lies, but the angel rises up on shaky knees, giving her hope.

After a couple of bumpy minutes, the familiar buildings start to take shape in the darkness around them. She can see the farmhouse with its lights on, but they turn away from it, angling instead toward the barn, lit only by a couple of exterior fires near which more of those Pioneers huddle. They come to attention as the truck approaches, shining its headlights on the barn door.

The smaller, standard-sized door built into the larger barn door opens, and another one of the strange nuns steps out, quickly shutting the door behind her. Up close, Roan can see her attire is even more bizarre than she first thought. She was right thinking about the Inquisition on her first glance. The nun's coat goes all the way down to her feet as she walks in big, dark boots. She's got those extra bits of sleeve hanging off her shoulders like a cowboy's duster, and leather gloves. Roan doesn't know the specific name of it, but the woman's head covering doesn't entirely shield her hair, revealing blond locks, a slender neck, and tight jawline. She looks like some edgy movie's interpretation of the Church in a dystopian future.

The nun and the armed men step aside, visibly deferring to Harrow, and then glancing over to her husband. Despite the fire in his eyes, he allows it. Roan knows his type; he'd rather let whatever is about to happen happen than challenge his wife in public. This way, he can still pretend it's all his idea. He can still hold on to the illusion of control.

"We're going to go inside," Harrow says to Roan. "Just you and me."

Roan feels a little robbed. If there really is a miracle behind those doors—the miracle she's been begging for without even knowing it, the miracle of a different kind of life—she wants to experience it alone, not with a passenger. She can't believe she believes these things; can't believe they've given her hope.

Hope. Curiosity. Interest. Emotions fluttering around inside her ribcage. She hasn't felt these in so long. She takes a step forward, but Harrow reaches out and puts a hand on the door, keeping it closed, and says, "Before we go in, I need to tell you something. Something about what you're about to see."

"The suspense is killing me," Roan says as a mask, an affect she hasn't quite shed. But she really means it. She really wants to know, *has* to know after hearing Nico's voice, after the light show, after their refusal to kill her. She pushes past Harrow before she can even speak, and into the barn. The building has been retrofitted, the stalls and loft cleared out, pews and an altar added. String lights snake around nearby poles and rafters above, and she can hear a generator hidden somewhere. A thick, red carpet leads down the center aisle and towards the altar, which has chairs, a podium, and a large crucifixion statue hanging above.

But it's what is on the altar, the *thing* in the center of the church. It can't be real. Maybe there was a celestial, if perfectly reasonable, explanation she didn't understand for the stars, but there was nothing that explained this other than she's simply gone insane, or the world has broken. Her eyes drift past the strange form at first, not really absorbing what it is she sees because it's so foreign, her brain unable to comprehend what she's looking at. But after a moment, she comes back because this thing has to be what Harrow meant she had to show her, not the church itself. As Roan looks at the shape on the altar, she finds she can't really explain what it is, can only really think of it in terms of what it *isn't*. It isn't really there, less like a concrete thing and more like an absence of something. It's like it's a black hole pulling everything in—light, sight, even, somehow, explanation, words themselves before they're even vocalized. It's like looking directly at the sun for too long, but it's her brain that can't handle it, not her eyes.

Roan realizes she's leaning against one of the pews to hold herself up, and as her legs liquify under her, she holds out her other hand, reaching for anything.

It's Harrow who comes to her aid, sliding under Roan's arm to hold her up. Roan is aware of her presence but cannot take her eyes off that strange hole in the world, desperate to make sense of it, to understand that this is supposed to be Columbia's miracle granter.

"Don't worry," Harrow says, snaking her arm around Roan's waist and pulling her so close she can feel the heat of her body. "I've got you."

"What is this?" Roan breathes. She wants to look away, to face Harrow, but she can't tear her eyes away. It's like she's being summoned to look at the thing, drawn to it. "*This thing* is an angel?"

"Just look, sweetheart," Harrow says, and Roan is so caught off guard by the seemingly innocuous pet name and the sudden desire to revel in it that it takes her a moment to realize that they are moving closer to the shape. "Just look at it."

Roan watches as the hole in the world begins to solidify, the absence taking physical form. Something roils inside that black hole, and just as Roan realizes she's looking at shimmering scarlet scales, a coil thicker than her torso rolls forth and spills out of the hole and into the world. It's followed by another and another and another, or maybe they're all part of the same great length—a gargantuan, serpentine mass not slithering but falling out into our world. There is no beginning and no end to the tangle, no heads or tails that Roan can see, just an endless thread of coils, a great big ball of scales the size of a minivan writhing before her. The noise the coils make is hypnotic, their great muscles pushing against one another, grinding against the altar, and Roan feels a strange longing of the kind she feels when she stands at the edge of a high place or next to a busy highway.

The urge to reach out and touch it.

No, not just touch it, but to step inside it.

To let the mass of coils consume her.

It's only when she tries to step toward it that she realizes Harrow has her arms wrapped around her, is holding her in place, and Roan feels a sudden anger for the woman who dares keep her from this goal she can't understand but knows she deeply needs.

"What is this?" Roan asks, realizing she's out of breath, trying to get closer. She's sweating. She needs this, maybe more than she's ever needed anything in her life. Even more than killing Garrett.

The coils answer for Harrow, unfurling from one another, falling away like a set of stage curtains revealing the action. Roan can see pieces of what the coils reveal before they fall away completely—porcelain skin, the sight of a shoulder, the edge of an ear, a green eye that's almost too bright. And just as she comes to realize what she's looking at, the coils fall away and show her everything.

Nico.

Or something that looks like Nico. Because Nico is dead, isn't she? Roan saw her die, had her blood all over her, feels it even still, and people don't come back to life, no matter what any book says.

And yet.

The Nico-shape stands up from its crouch, its pose triumphant and vast and unashamed in its nudity. She looks down at Roan, who has fallen to her knees in sudden supplication, Harrow by her side, holding onto her in a protective stance that Roan wants to think about, but she is so inundated with information, so completely overloaded by the impossible figure that stands before her. Nico is nude, her stomach flat, unaffected by the pregnancy Roan knew her with. Her legs, pelvis, and underarms are marked with wisps of unshaven hair.

But not her head.

Her hair is made of snakes, each one of them a Medusa coil whose serpentine face is turned towards Roan.

"Oh, God," Roan gasps, not knowing if it's an exasperation or an invocation.

The Nico-shape steps forward, coming down the altar as the massive coils roil around her like waves, spinning and churning, becoming ecstatic at her presence. They thread around the altar, surrounding Roan and Harrow, forming a wall, blocking the men from witnessing whatever is about to happen.

"Nico..." Roan crawls forward on all fours, bringing Harrow unexpectedly with her. Roan kneels before the thing that looks like Nico, the thing she wants to be Nico, and holds up her hands. She opens her mouth, but she doesn't know what to say, because no words are enough. How could they ever be? She simply stands there, slack-jawed, feeling idiotic.

Feeling.

And then the Nico-shape reaches out and takes her chin in its hand.

And with its other hand, its puts its fingers into Roan's mouth.

She wants to say something, anything, but the entity forces its fingers further back, deeper, puts its hand into her, and Roan knows she should be gagging, but she doesn't. She knows she should feel uncomfortable, should feel pain, as not only the fingers but the hand, the wrist, the forearm, the elbow, slide down into her, but all she feels is warmth. Like a gulp of hot chocolate on a cold night. All she feels is connection. Nico handing her that very cup, coming to sit next to her, to lay her warmth against her. Roan feels the shape's coils coming closer, and then wrapping themselves around her legs, her arms, holding her still and then holding her up, lifting her from the ground entirely, lifting her towards the sky like she's a thing to be worshipped. The Nico-thing enters her through her mouth, but not just her mouth. The coils hold Roan tight, they spread her wide, and she doesn't know which part of the Nico-shaped-thing is going inside her, but there's something entering her through her ass, her pussy, thin slivers sliding into her ears as the bulk of this entity slides down Roan's throat, and she welcomes all of it. She welcomes the warmth, the feeling, the righteousness, as everything she's ever wanted to feel slowly pushes into her at once. She feels the desire for revenge fulfilled. She feels justice. She feels the love of Nico, of Harrow, a completion of a kind she's never felt before as she takes the entity and all of its coils inside her.

"It's a miracle," Harrow says from somewhere around her.

But no, no, Roan doesn't think that's true. It's not a miracle. It's something else. What's the opposite of a miracle?

This is a calamity.

Such a delicious calamity. A revelation in bright neon.

PART 3:

THE SECOND COMING

MESSIAH

The light wakes her, but she does not open her eyes. Like a child before school, Roan holds them shut, turns in her half-sleep away from the source of the light, trying to squeeze in just a few more minutes of sleep, of unconsciousness, of blissful unawareness, before being forced back into the world. She exists like that for a moment, in an empty state of half-dark, returning to sleep her only desire. She wonders if this is how a child in the womb feels when it's time to be born.

And with that image, that question, the world comes crashing back over her. She has those moments of struggle everyone has when waking, lying there and remembering what's a memory and what's reality. Child. Womb. Nico. Dead. Gone. Blood. Revenge. Garrett. More blood. Capture.

The thing in the barn.

Return?

Roan's breath comes arrhythmical, and her heart spikes in her chest. She twitches in bed, partially kicking herself free of the covers. She knows these are memories, not dreams, that whatever happened to her—*that thing tunneling into her through her mouth*—is real. There is the initial shock, the memory of the reality in which something like that could exist, but Roan isn't as frightened as logic tells her—as she *feels*—she ought to be. The presence of the thing in the barn, the memory of how it looked, like a dark kaleidoscope, of it becoming something out of nothing, of it looking like Nico, of it entering her body, doesn't seem so strange, though everything about what she just thought tells her it very much should be.

For a moment, Roan suspects that the old survival mechanism is at play again, her body and mind shutting down nonessential functions, like emotions, in order for her to survive. But this feels different than before, different than after her high school boyfriend was killed in a drunk driving accident or after her grandma had that stroke. Different than the times she wondered if she'd have enough to make rent, to eat. Different than when Nico died or when she killed Garrett. It is like that, but it is also not that. It's something *more*. It's like she is somehow able to move beyond those distressing emotions. Not because of a desperation to free herself from them, but through something like evolution.

No, not evolution.

Symbiosis.

Something is inside your body, Roan tells herself. Because it must still be there. But then she wonders, is that it? Is that really what happened to her? Eyes still closed, she focuses on feeling her body, on being present, on the mindfulness so many therapists made her try that she absolutely hated because none of them could ever explain it right and just spoke about it like it was an instant cure-all for every one of her problems. Just focus on one thing at a time, she tells herself, feeling herself lying on her side, feeling the blankets wrapping her, pulled tight like when her mother would tuck her in as a child, before she knew what Roan really was, before she threw her out into the world. She feels her right arm, forearm laid across her hip, hand draping down to her stomach. Something about her feels different than before, different in a way she doesn't know how to describe yet because she doesn't have all the information. She breathes, trying to feel her presence in her body, but she is distracted by a shifting somewhere beyond her.

"She's awake!" whispers a voice from somewhere in the room. It's followed by a series of quiet shushes, those sibilant S-noises snaking their way through the air. Roan feels herself twitch and knows she cannot hide her wakefulness anymore. She opens her eyes slowly, pretending, at least, to be sleepier than she is.

Roan notices first that she's not alone. Scattered throughout the room are many of the nuns she recognizes from around the property. A handful of them are standing looking down at her in anticipation, like children eager to wake their parents on Christmas morning. But a great many more of the women are scattered about the floor, on their knees, hands clasped in prayer. A couple of them are even crying with happiness.

After she takes in the women, the rest of the room comes into focus. She's in a large bedroom, and judging by the country decor interior, she thinks she's inside the farmhouse. She's lying in a large bed, a thin sheet draped over her, the window open, letting in a warm summer breeze. There's a quilt-draped chair in the corner of the room, a dresser, a vanity—all the furniture looking like it was made by hand long ago, not bought and assembled using wordless visual instructions. From what she's seen in the rest of the property, she's surprised at the lack of religious iconography. Only a small crucifix affixed above the doorway.

Roan knows she should feel scared or at the very least alarmed. Startled. *Something*. She thinks of the facts. She just killed a man, someone who appeared to be a respected member of this closed-off religious community. She was taken into custody, brought before... *something*. A presence. She doesn't know why, but she doesn't feel comfortable calling it a monster. Despite its actions, Roan doesn't feel like what it was trying to do was harm her. It didn't even make her feel truly afraid, and yet it was undoubtedly something not human. Something that emerged from a black hole in the form of a writhing ball of enormous snakes. Something that looked like Nico. A thing that then crawled inside her, only for her to wake from it all not in her own bed but in this new one, surrounded by a cloister of nuns.

And yet she feels calm. She feels settled. She feels—she doesn't want to think it for fear of jinxing herself—*safe*?

Roan hears movement in the hallway beyond the room, and suddenly that brunette woman, Harrow, is there in the doorway. Same oversized glasses, same sandals, different sundress. Is it a new day?

"You're awake," Harrow says with awe. She moves toward Roan, and the nuns make way for her, moving aside quickly as if they dare not taint her with their touch. Harrow grabs a rocking chair from beside the bed and pulls it closer, scraping the runners against the hardwood. She places her hands on the mattress, close to—but not touching—Roan. "You've been asleep for three days. How are you feeling?"

How is she feeling? What a loaded question. How can she be feeling everything and yet nothing? How does that make sense? How is she supposed to explain that? She opens her mouth but has no idea what she's going to say, so she shuts it again. What words can possibly be enough?

"It's okay," Harrow says, patting Roan on the arm with just her fingertips. Careful, tentative, watching to see if Roan flinches, if she'll allow a touch. Roan allows it, wants to allow her more than such a simple touch, but thinks such a thought would be a betrayal of Nico's memory. "Would you like me to help you sit up?"

Roan nods, feeling inexplicably safe around this woman. She pushes herself up onto her elbows as Harrow grabs an armful of pillows from the quilt-covered chair, the closest nuns coming to help. As Roan moves, she listens to her body, and it sounds different. It feels different. It feels like she's more inside herself, more aware of herself. She feels like she did when she started taking hormones, when she stopped intentionally pulling her consciousness out of her body. She feels herself as a weight she's never felt before. She thinks she needs to feel herself, examine herself with more of her senses, and she looks down over herself as Harrow and the nuns help her into a sitting position.

"There's a good girl."

At the praise, Roan can feel her heart quicken, and she's pulled away from the realization she was headed towards. Something lights inside her, a fire she hasn't felt for a long time. A fire that feels like being alive. She looks up at Harrow, who looks down at her over the rim of her huge glasses, which have slipped slightly down her nose. Her hand is on Roan's shoulder, squeezing tenderly, and Roan's delight at that touch is another knife in the memory of Nico.

Tell me again, Roan wants to say. It takes energy for her to keep her hands by her side, to not reach up and clutch at Harrow, to beg for more of those beautiful words. *Please, tell me again how good I've been.* She can't explain why, but she suddenly, desperately, needs to hear it, needs to feel the feeling those words give her, to drink their delicious life. But instead of begging, she squirms, and in moving her legs she can feel the rest of her body, feel the weight she's become, the gravity. She looks away from Harrow, down at herself, and that's when she sees it.

The unmistakable swell of her stomach.

She gasps, a huge gulp of air, and she kicks her legs, freeing herself from the sheet but not dispelling the illusion. Because it's not an illusion. It's reality. Roan grabs the bottom of the large, pink nightshirt—brain skipping over the fact that it is not hers, mentally bookmarking for later the fear that someone else has examined her body, might know who and what she really is. She hauls the nightshirt up and looks down at the fertile bulge of her stomach. She feels feelings again, everything at once crashing down on her—fear, surprise, the sense of impossibility. A recollection of the Nico she knew and then the writhing ball of snakes. Nico with her snake hair and the coils pushing their way down Roan's throat and into her body, but not just her throat, her every gleefully awaiting orifice, and just as it all seems like it's going to be too much to bear, Harrow is sitting by her side, one hand on Roan's belly, the other on her shoulder.

"Look at me," she says, not urgently. Calmly. Low. The voice of a lover in the dark, whispering endless promises. And Roan does, looking away from her stomach and into Harrow's eyes, feeling a single chip come out of the massive weight of her panic. But it's a chip that starts an avalanche.

"What did you do to me?" she asks, even though she wonders who it really was, this woman, this place, or that thing.

"We didn't do anything," Harrow says, smiling. There are tears brimming in her eyes. They fall when she tries to blink them away. "Our miracle-giver isn't in the barn anymore. They are in *you*."

Roan is aware of a muttering all around her and looks over Harrow's shoulder to see the room full of nuns are now all kneeling, each one of them, all facing her. They have their hands clasped before them. Some of them look down to the floor while others turn their faces up towards Roan. A couple even have arms extended, as if they desire not just to look upon her but to touch her. They mutter quietly to themselves, but she can hear their praise, and she delights in it.

II: SACRED

PART 4:

Jezebel

WITHOUT FORM, AND VOID

When Roan sat in the hospital chapel after It Happened, she almost wished there had been blood on her hands. She wished there had been some sort of mark, something she could've taken with her. Something that proved any of it had been real.

All she had was her memories.

All she had was her anger.

And the thought that nothing else would ever fill her again.

PROPHET

Roan is surrounded by a hive of nuns, but their edges are as soft as they were before. They are not dressed like they're prepared for a post-apocalyptic road war, like the first one she saw. They're all wearing nothing but simple white shifts that look handmade, without head coverings or shoes, treading now in a holy place. They surround Roan, hovering around her like little woodland animals to her fairy princess, every moment at her beck and call, helping dress her, do her make-up, her hair. They peel away everything she used to be and replace it all with something new, something she didn't know she could be.

There was a moment before Roan collected herself, a moment just after she realized someone had changed her clothes, where she wondered if these women *knew*. If, upon closer examination of her body, they could tell she hadn't been born like them. Her surgery was complete, but she'd been clocked before and was accepting of the fact she very likely would be again. And yet if any of these nuns truly knew about her, they said nothing, continuing their praise of this newly revealed Roan every step of the way.

And as much as Roan delights in their praise, she can feel the shape inside her delighting in it even more. She can feel it squirming in a way that somehow transcends physicality, a movement not in her body but in her soul—if there is such a thing. There's a part of her that wonders if what she is experiencing is a possession, but she denies it. She's in control of herself, but she's not alone. Whatever this is, it feels instead like a symbiosis, a cohabitation, like when angler fish mate and the male physically fuses himself with the female.

Who are you? Roan wonders. *What are you?* The responses she gets are not entirely answers, and they do not come in words but in feelings. Feelings that are not her own projected inside her head. Simple things like *safe*, *warm*, *home*. The rudimentary thoughts of a child, even though she knows that's not what is inside her.

She tries to decode these thoughts as she sits in a chair in a guest room, in front of an enormous, full-length mirror, the kind that ought to be in a castle. A huge, ornate frame sitting fully on the floor, taking up half the wall. The mirror allows her to witness her slow transformation under the steadily working fingers of the nuns. They'd offered to bathe her, but Roan refused, cleaning the mud and dirt and Garrett's blood off alone in one of the farmhouse's enormous guest bathrooms. While inside, she stood naked before the mirror, staring at herself and the round swell of her belly.

I should be horrified, she thought. Anyone who saw her on the street would think she was ready to give birth at any moment. It wasn't just her stomach that had changed, but the rest of her body too. She'd gained pregnancy weight, could see it in her arms and face, and in the way she would gain weight after she started HRT, in her hips, her upper arms, her tits. *I should be scared*. But instead, all she felt, all she continues to feel, is solace. She feels the way she felt when it was just her and Nico on a Sunday morning, lying in bed, not a care in the world, not a need to go anywhere except occasional trips to the kitchen, and—due to Nico's belly—more frequent trips to the bathroom. Completely safe. Cocooned. The presence inside Roan was reassuring, had her convinced that no harm would come to her.

When she emerged from the bathroom, the nuns were there, ready. They bleached the purple from her hair, stripping that and some of the black, leaving Roan's hair a gray-white she actually found herself quite fond of. They trimmed her nails and plucked her eyebrows, and Roan tensed under their touch until she finally relaxed when they saw her discomfort and told her how well she was doing.

"We're almost done," Harrow says, coming to check on her as they pumice the callouses from her heels and brush the knots out of her hair. Roan thinks about how they say the hurt is supposed to be good for you, how suffering builds character. "You're being a very good girl."

Roan unclenches at the complement, more than she thinks she ought to, more than she thinks was possible. She feels the same kind of relaxation she did after taking a shot or sinking into a hot bath, the warmth relieving her muscles. The presence inside her feels the same thing. It squirms with delight, and Roan can feel it, in its wordless way, asking for more. More praise. Like sustenance. Ambrosia.

"I am?" she finds herself asking, reveling in it, wanting to hear it not just again, but especially from Harrow, wanting it just as much as the passenger inside her.

"Yes," says Harrow, patting Roan's shoulder. "Very good. We want you to look your best for when the television people come."

Roan remembers what Harrow said during her preaching, something about people coming to Columbia to listen to the word of the miracles, to spread them, to prove their veracity.

"I'm going to be on TV?"

Harrow nods.

"Oh, no, no," Roan shakes her head. "No, I can't do that."

"Yes, you can," Harrow says, gently placing a hand on the top of her head. Her touch freezes Roan, and she wants to push into it, like a cat begging for pets. As if Harrow hears this thought, she gently slides her hand down the side of Roan's head, brushing her newly-pale hair, gracing her cheeks, her neck, and Roan thinks this is what it should've felt like, should've looked like, when Harrow's husband touched her. "I know you can."

Roan chastises herself, apologizes to Nico, even though she's sure she can't hear her, for feeling what she feels at this woman's touch, at her praise. Nico is dead. Roan is supposed to hurt and to keep hurting in her absence. That hurt is supposed to prove her love was real, to pave the way for some sort of salvation for her. Isn't it?

No.

The voice is sudden and definitive and not her own, and it knows, oh, it *knows* this is not the truth. The hurt doesn't mean anything; it only hurts. There is reason to feel it, but no reason to seek it.

"This is like nothing we've ever experienced," Harrow says. "Never before has it chosen anyone like this, has it inhabited anyone like this."

"Not even you?" Roan asks, feeling bad for putting Harrow on the spot like that. She would've thought the face of the religious community would be number one on the list of hosts for... whatever is living with Roan now.

Harrow shakes her head.

"When we first found the angel, it looked unformed. Maybe it was weak. To me, it looked like a bubbling mass, like a small geyser in the dirt leaking dark fluid. But even then, I felt it. I knew what it was, that it was special." She puts her hand on Roan's shoulder. "In the same way I know you're special."

Roan reaches up and touches Harrow's hand, gently, not entirely innocently, and she feels a sense of forgiveness washing over her, of allowance. It is from her but also the thing inside her, telling her this feeling is okay, that it is not forbidden, despite what she still feels for Nico.

When the nuns finally finish with her, Roan sits up straight and looks across the room at her own reflection, nearly unrecognizable. Gone is her dark lipstick, her eyeshadow. Her lips are now a soft, rosy pink, matching the rouge they applied to her cheeks. Her straightened hair frames her face like misty curtains, a face that's covered by a thin veil. They've dressed her in a shawl of robin's egg blue above an immaculate white dress that does something optical to emphasize the roundness of her tummy. She's barefoot. The whole thing reminds her of the portraits of saints she used to see in her Sunday school books.

"How do you feel?" Harrow asks when Roan's transformation is finally complete. To be honest, she has no idea how she feels because she feels too many things at once. But she does, in fact, feel. Things have shaken loose inside her, and she's trying to understand them again, how they all work.

"I don't... know," Roan says, looking at herself in the mirror. Her reflection looks strange in a way she can't identify, like some other Roan is looking back out at her from a parallel dimension. She turns her head at various angles, taking herself in, trying to find some flaw, some imperfection that will reveal this reflection's identity or the source of this forgery, but there is none. She looks... *evolved*.

Slowly, unused to the extra weight she now carries, Roan stands from the chair. She doesn't know how, but she feels taller. Like the world has ceased folding in on her and now she's pushing it out and away, finally forcing it to make room for her. In the mirror, holding her belly, she looks even more like a portrait of a saint.

"How do I look?" Roan says, looking at Harrow through her reflection in the mirror.

"You look beautiful," says Harrow, and Roan feels too many things—a thump in her chest, a fluttering heartbeat of something long dead stirring to life again. And a pang of guilt. "It's okay to feel good about it," Harrow says, noticing the conflict on Roan's face. She doesn't get it entirely, but she gets most of it. "The feeling of worship is strange," Harrow says. "Trust me, I know." She gestures to Roan's belly. "But worship is what brings gods into the world."

MY BODY

Roan has seen all the classic films that quickly come to mind in this situation. *Rosemary's Baby. The Brood. The Omen.* The stories that make pregnancy and children scary. She's seen all the possession movies, stories where an innocent young woman—always a woman, always a girl—is inhabited by a terrible demonic force.

This doesn't feel anything like any of those. But *why* doesn't it feel like that?

This premise is familiar to her. But her reaction is not. *Pregnant* isn't even the word Roan would use to describe herself. Whatever happened to her, it happened without the intervention of a man or even a penis. Neither is *possessed* correct. There is something inside her, and she guesses she would call that something *alive,* but it is not so simple as biology, and it's obvious that that's how everyone else feels as well.

Roan sits at the head of the large table in the farmhouse's side yard, the groups of nuns milling about her. They made sure to sit her underneath the most shaded part of the overhanging trellis, made sure the sun dare not mar her skin. Roan wears a simple white dress and has no shoes on. Harrow helped her pull her hair up into a bun, not because Roan really needed any help, but because she wanted it. She wanted to be waited on, but especially by Harrow, to feel her hands in her hair, feel her toes curl as Harrow's fingertips graced the back of her neck, pulling up the loose hairs.

This want still feels like a betrayal when Roan thinks of Nico. Harrow had dropped her hands down onto Roan's shoulders when she'd finished doing her hair, and then came closer, peering over Roan's shoulder to her bulging belly, telling her that she needed to eat something, that she needed to stay strong.

Which is how Roan found herself sitting at the outside table, a feast laid out before her. Food of all kinds, from flanks of ham so fresh they must've come from this property's very own pigs to fresh glasses of milk and ripe, succulent fruit.

The nuns have brought her everything she can imagine, but despite their adoration, Roan only has eyes for Harrow. She sits to her right, watching her intently, making sure nothing is out of place. Roan doesn't think she's taken an eye off her since she sat down.

Is this how you felt when I told you I adored you? Is this how you felt when I knelt at your feet?

Roan tries to make it look like she's not looking at Harrow, but she knows she fails. She looks out over the feast, but her eyes keep darting back to the woman.

"Is everything okay?" Harrow asks, her voice suddenly rising.

Yes, Roan thinks, but does not know how to say. What she wants is not just the food itself, but for it to be brought to her. For the action. The worship. For that feeling of adoration to come and overtake her, to push away all those questions rolling about in her head.

Harrow must take Roan's silence as a negative, because she suddenly reaches across the table for a fork. She stabs it into a slice of pie and lifts it to her mouth.

"It's okay," she says, more to herself than to Roan, who sees the fork in her hand, the bits of crust and cherry stuck to the tines. How is she supposed to ask for something like this? How is she supposed to ask for something as simple as what she wants?

It feels... humiliating in a way she was not at all prepared for, to ask for her needs to be met at no cost to someone else.

"Do you want to try it?" Harrow asks, gesturing with the fork, and there's a pleading in her voice that Roan feels reflected in her mind. She needs for Roan to try it, for Roan to like it, needs for Roan to lavish praise back on her just as much as this new Roan needs praise from Harrow.

Does she want to try it? *Yes. Yes, please, yes*, Roan thinks, aching for it, finally seeing her opening without having to feel the unexpected shame of asking. She says nothing but wets her lips and opens her mouth just slightly, looking Harrow in the eyes as she does. She can see it the moment it hits, Harrow's understanding. The reason for her hesitation clicks in Harrow's mind, and she knows now what her goddess wants. She sticks the fork into the pie and pulls it back out, scooting closer to Roan, who opens her mouth. Harrow comes closer, refusing to allow Roan to even bend, and gently slides the fork between her lips. Roan doesn't allow herself to open wider, feels the moist piece of pie brush against her lips, her tongue. Harrow holds her other hand out, under Roan's chin, to catch any dropped crumbs, but there are none. Roan shuts her eyes as she closes her lips around the fork, and Harrow slowly, delicately, slides the utensil free.

Roan doesn't think anything in her life has ever felt so goddamn good.

The first night, Roan slept in the guest room she woke up in, but ever since, she's slept in a bed more magnificent than any she has ever owned. It's four-postered, with a lush canopy spread out above the mattress, translucent veils dangling down to the floor. It looks like a bed from a fairy tale. Roan's slept in some that came close to this regalia, passing out after strenuous sex in apartments or condos that were far too rich for her. Just like this. She feels like she doesn't belong here, the woman who stole ash trays and watches and loose jewelry from those same bedrooms while their oblivious owners slept soundly after what they put each other's bodies through. Roan knows she doesn't need to do the same here. She knows they'll simply give her those things if she asks. Not that she even wants those things anymore. Her desires, like the rest of her, have evolved.

"I'd be honored if you'd take it," Harrow says, gesturing to the room.

Roan spends a long time looking at the room, the bed, wondering, not knowing why.

"Please," Harrow puts her hands on Roan's shoulders and guides her across the room. "You deserve it." The words hit her like a whipcrack, and she doesn't know why. "Here, let me help you." Harrow guides Roan over to the bed, turning her so she can sit her down. Roan is perfectly able to turn around and sit down on her own, but the feeling of Harrow's hands on her, guiding her, does something to her, makes her legs shake.

Harrow bends down as she helps Roan to get seated, and then she keeps going, moving down to Roan's bare feet. Roan gasps, tucks her feet in, hiding them.

"It's all right," Harrow says. "I won't hurt you." She holds there for a moment, waiting for Roan to move, to allow her to touch her again, and she does, gently unclenching. Harrow reaches out and takes Roan's right foot gingerly, as if she's holding something soft and breakable. She takes the left and lifts Roan's legs up, gently massaging the bottoms of her feet as she slides them under the covers and into b
ed.

Roan feels heat blast up her body and in between her legs. She had something she wanted to ask, and Harrow's fingers make it difficult, even as she lifts the blanket and pulls it over Roan.

"Get some rest," Harrow says. "I'll come back to check on you later." She moves to leave but is stopped by Roan's fingers around her wrist. Roan doesn't realize she's grabbed her, but she cannot let go. She reaches out with her other hand and holds Harrow, traps her there on the bed. She wants to ask, is afraid to ask, and certainly afraid to order, even though something tells her Harrow would obey any order Roan gives, even the slightest suggestion. All she can do is shake her head, her throat locked up.

"You want me to stay with you?" Harrow asks.

Roan nods quickly.

"Okay." Harrow pats Roan on the hand. She takes her glasses off her face and sets them down on the bedside table. She gets up, but only to cross the room and close the door, kicking her sandals off along the way. When she returns, she looks down at Roan. "Where?"

Roan pulls the sheet aside and turns over, pointing her swollen belly away from Harrow.

Harrow slides in behind Roan, wrapping an arm around her.

"You're such a brave girl," she says, holding Roan tight. Roan very nearly flinches at the words. She doesn't know if she can take any more of them, and yet she yearns for them. Harrow continues singing her praises, telling Roan everything she's always wanted to hear while Roan silently cries, her head turned away into the dark, wondering if it is okay to love after your love has died.

DEFIANCE

It isn't until long after Roan has fallen asleep, what feels both like hours and not enough time at all of Harrow listening to the soft rhythm of her breathing, that she finally forces herself to get up and leave, to attend to her many chores. She finds Paxton standing outside, waiting for her, to corner her. Corner her? Why does she think of it like that, like he's a predator and she something in his sights?

Because that's how it is. That's how he's always thought of you, she tells herself in that strange, intrusive voice that's been perking up lately, the one that told her to roll over, to get on top of Paxton in their bed. The one that sounds like Roan.

Harrow tries to remember what it was like when they first met, when they first fell for one another. She recalls Paxton sitting atop his horse, looking like a glorious cowboy out of American myth, the kind of man she was told by so many people that she should love, that every woman should love, and she supposed she did for a while—or at least she thought she did. How else would she explain looking at his small barbarisms, the casual cruelty of his words, and her excusing all of them? How else would she explain how she became more like him, the way people often become like one another in the beginning of relationships (except he never became more like her, never took on her kindness, her softness, and she only absorbed his cruelty, his apathy)?

Brainwashing. That's how. Not just by Paxton, but by this country, this place that wants her to be a woman, which, to them, is not a person.

Harrow wonders why recalling the beginning of their relationship is suddenly so important to her. Not the existence of the moment itself, but its recollection, the resurrection of those feelings.

You know why. It's because her thoughts and feelings about her husband have changed, because there's something different between them now. She knows why the word she thought of moments ago was *resurrection.*

It's because those feelings are dead.

Harrow thinks all this, but all she does is smile as she stops before Paxton, on the outside, the obedient wife.

"I don't like this," he says, matter-of-factly, as if his displeasure will be all that's needed to shut everything down. And it might have been, once upon a time. Maybe even as recently as a couple weeks ago. A couple days. But things are different now. They've changed, as Harrow has changed yet again. And yet again, Paxton has stayed the same. When Harrow says nothing, when it's clear to Paxton that he needs to elaborate more, he does. "I don't like this woman," he says. "I don't like these TV people coming here. They're all outsiders."

"Yes," Harrow says just as matter-of-factly, as if to challenge him with her indifference to his plight. *Indifference?* she thinks. *Should a wife be so indifferent to her husband's suffering?* But isn't that what Paxton always talks about? Redemptive suffering? *Salvifici doloris.* This suffering is supposed to make a person better. And yet when faced with it, he wants nothing to do with it. As if it's meant for everyone else, not him.

Those two forces, two voices, scream at one another inside her, the one that wants her to sit down and obey, and the one that wants to do nothing but fly free, be freer than she's ever been in her life. Harrow thought she had her life, everyone's life in Columbia, completely figured out, the presence of the angelic entity in the barn finally solidifying everything. She thought she knew everything, though after a few minutes of admitted concern in the wake of Garrett's death, she now feels surer than ever. It's hard to believe that she ever doubted Roan, that for a moment Harrow thought she ought to be punished for what she'd done to Garrett. Now she can't imagine anything or anyone hurting the angel's vessel, seeks only her praise, her adoration. Someone she thought she would hold a vendetta against she wants more than ever to please.

"She's…" Harrow struggles to come up with the words, because what words will do Roan justice? There aren't any, she thinks, daydreaming of Roan's long, silvery hair, of her hands in Harrow's, bowed in supplication. She thinks of the grace of her bare feet on the grass and the touch of her lips under Harrow's fingers.

Harrow's train of thought hits a bump. Is that… what she thinks of? Roan's *lips*?

"The TV people," Paxton says, his voice stern, "they're coming here to talk about this place and its miracles." When he talks, he points at the ground, enunciating and emphasizing each syllable as if he can make himself clearer. "About the angel. Not… her."

"She *is* one of the miracles," Harrow says, and the more she says it out loud, the more she knows it's true, the more she recognizes this feeling breaching up from deep within her, because it's the feeling everyone told her she should feel for Paxton.

"Are you going to let her do this?" Paxton asks, the challenge clear. She can't imagine feeling that feeling for him now. Standing before her, he looks small, and she can't believe she ever bowed before him.

"It's not my choice," Harrow says. "It's not your choice, and it's not her choice. She's *been chosen*. She's the very miracle they're coming to see."

"But she isn't one of us."

A sudden thought strikes Harrow, a question delivered to her mind as if by divine provenance.

"What do you see when you look at it?"

"What?"

"The angel," Harrow says, "What do you see when you look at it?"

Paxton takes a deep breath. He's told her this before, monologued this at her before, but she wants to hear it again, wants to hear his zeal, his surety.

"A tidal wave," he says. "I see a foamy, white wave that is still, but is also somehow moving. It's sweeping everywhere, flowing over the whole world, and its swept us up inside it—Columbia—and we are buoyed up on its crest into someplace new."

Harrow knows the rest, she knows what happens to those who aren't lifted up by the wave, and as she recalls the horror of those souls drowning beneath that white water, she walks away from her husband with a suddenness that surprises even herself, carrying with her a feeling she knows not just how to describe but how to finally name with absolute clarity.

PART 5:

DEICIDE

SPREADING THE WORD

Days later, Harrow flies around the property like a banshee trying to get everyone into place, trying to get everything fixed, all set up for their visitors. The nuns and a great many of the other Columbia parishioners help her with cleaning the house, mowing the lawn, and tending to the gardens while she goes back to Roan every five minutes to check on her.

Is that it? Harrow asks herself. *Are you really checking on her? Merely doing your duty? Or are you just looking for any excuse to see her again?* She knows the answer to those questions, and it's the devil on her shoulder that whispers them to her.

It's like love. It's beyond love. You love her. And in a way you know you've never loved your husband.

Harrow's stressed and excited at the same time. Nervous and flighty. But she can handle it. This is important. Maybe the most important thing that's ever happened. They're about to share their miracles with the world.

Harrow notices that Paxton is nowhere to be found. He's been spending more and more time with his Pioneers lately, shirking his duties as a leader of Columbia and husband to Harrow. He hasn't made love to her since Roan arrived. There's a part of Harrow that wants to feel bad about that, but there isn't a part that actually does. If she's being honest, she's hardly noticed. She only thinks about it when she's outside of Roan's presence and her thoughts are a little freer to wander.

"They're here." Harrow doesn't entirely realize who says it—one of the nuns—because she's peeling off from giving the living room one final sweep and sailing down the front steps of the house to meet the television crew in the front drive.

They've arrived in an old, black panel van, the driver a baby-faced young man in a suit that looks a size too big for him. His partner is much bigger, stockier, the kind of build that suggests he grew up on a farm. The young man takes his suit jacket off in the summer heat and tosses it back into the van as Harrow comes down to greet them.

The side of their van says SPOOKLIGHT SOCIETY in stylized letters, a mysterious orange light among the trees of a swamp behind the word.

None of the so-called "serious" national news stations agreed to cover Columbia's miracles. Harrow didn't reach out to any of the local channels in Parthas either after they joined in on running slanderous pieces about Columbia. But that's okay with her. There was never any great change in the world that everyone universally agreed upon the moment it happened. Heliocentrism, evolution. If it takes the word of an amateur, ghost- and miracle-chasing crew to get the word out, then that's what it takes.

"Mrs. Harrow?" the driver calls to her, shielding his eyes against the light. In their correspondence, he agreed to refer to Harrow by her first name, but it seems he hasn't dropped the formality entirely.

"That's me," she says, descending the steps and holding out her hand. "Chris, I presume."

"That's me," Chris Bauman says, offering his own hand. "This is Shaun, my righthand man."

"Ma'am." Shaun nods politely, already opening the van's sliding door and rooting around for supplies.

"It's nice to finally meet you in person," Chris says, looking around, and Harrow knows exactly who he's looking for.

"She's not here," she says, and then adds, "I mean right now. She's just resting, preparing for the interview."

"Totally cool," Chris says. "We weren't planning on jumping straight into that anyway. We wanted to talk with you first, get some shots of the property, that sort of thing."

"Of course, you're welcome to explore any area of Columbia you desire," Harrow says, distractedly looking over Chris's shoulder at what Shaun is moving around in the back of the van. She sees some of what she expects: cameras, tripods, and sound equipment. But there are also what appear to be props. Without realizing she's doing it, Harrow steps past Chris and is suddenly behind Shaun, looking into the van. It looks like a Halloween store. There are battery-powered candles, tiny effigies made out of sticks, and old, leatherbound books. Blackout curtains. Foam tombstones. Pop culture references; versions of the *Necronomicon*, the Aklo-to-English dictionary, and the *Dux ad Ignotus*. Harrow knows the Latin name of the Guide to the Unknown, an infamous tome that was said to be used in ancient witch hunts.

"What is all this?" she asks.

"Oh. It's just set dressing," the young man says. "We use it for a lot of our shoots. It's no big deal."

Harrow feels something inside of her light up, a fire she has only felt in small bursts before, one that's grown ever stronger and louder in the presence of Roan. The devil on her shoulder bursts into flame with glee.

Is this truly it? Harrow wonders. *Is this how people are supposed to feel? They say it makes you stronger. Does it feel like this?* She's never felt such a thing coming from her feelings for Paxton.

"We won't need any of that," she says. It's quick. It's concise. It's without a stutter or a hitch. It's a command, like the kind Roan speaks, and she knows the moment she utters it that it's going to be obeyed.

To confirm, Chris nervously says, "Sure! No problem."

"Why don't you bring your equipment inside," Harrow says, her tone matronly again but still confident and strong, "and we'll get started?"

"Yes, ma'am," Chris says, hurrying over to the van to help Shaun out, and Harrow wonders, *Is this how your power feels?*

SCHISM

It's strange how quickly things can change, Roan thinks as she sits in a rocking chair on the back porch of the farmhouse, waiting. It was only a couple weeks ago she was filled with rage, so consumed it seemed like there was nothing else in the world. There *was* nothing else in the world, her world. Nothing but the inevitability of Andrew Garrett's blood on her hands. An endgame whose aftermath she did not prepare for.

But now there's something. Now there's some*one*.

But which one of them are you thinking about? Roan asks herself. She looks out over the fields of Columbia, her hands rubbing her growing belly. Instead of rage, now she's filled with... she doesn't really know what to call it, it's been such a long time since she felt it. It can't be peace, can it? She's never even dreamed of such a feeling. Not since Nico.

Roan turns as the screen door swings open and Harrow walks out.

"Hello, sweetheart," she says, and Roan feels that same flutter in her chest whenever Harrow dotes on her. She comes over and sits on the porch railing, putting a hand on Roan's shoulder. There's something different about her. Something brighter than she's seen on her face before, even yesterday. A calmness. A surety, like nothing in the world can knock her off her perch. She looks down at Roan over her big glasses, and Roan sees a new light in her eyes. "How are you?"

Roan reaches up and takes Harrow's hand and gently squeezes it. She's nervous in a way she didn't expect. Nervous in the way she was when she first met Nico, when she first realized *holy shit, this girl is actually flirting with me.* Roan had always been a bit of a flirt with everyone she knew, and it hadn't been until Nico started giving it back that she realized she'd started something, and that something was real. Now, here with Harrow, she realizes she's started something again. But she can't help but wonder, is what Harrow feels for her because of her or because of what she carries?

"I'm okay," Roan says aloud, still not entirely sure what all that means or how to voice it. She's under no immediate threat right now, is what she really means, but she doesn't think she's really *okay*. Not yet anyway.

"There's my girl," Harrow says. She pulls herself up off the railing and kneels before Roan, gives her hair a last-minute finger-brush. "They're here, waiting just inside. Are you ready to talk to them?"

They're here. And not just here, but here specifically for her. They're here because she's special, and they want to tell the rest of the world about her. The attention of Harrow and the nuns is one thing, something that makes Roan feel equally beautiful and uncomfortable, but with these new people, with the idea of the whole world looking at her, she can feel the scales beginning to tip.

Roan realizes Harrow's hands are in her lap, in her own hands, and she holds them tight.

No, I don't want to talk to them, she thinks. *I only want you. I just want it to be you and me and no one else in the world except this life inside me. For you to tell me I'm beautiful and I'm sweet and strong and loved, and I'm so sorry I feel this way, Nico, but I can't help it. I need you to forgive me, to not hate me for saying I'd wait around, I'd stay alone, and I'd try to meet you wherever you've gone. I'm a liar. I lied to you, to your memory, to your ghost and the ghost of the life inside you.*

After a long time, Roan says "I'm ready, if you'll stay with me."

Harrow squeezes her hands back, and then Roan is absolutely sure her heart stops for a moment as Harrow lifts those hands to her lips and kisses them. Her lips brush so gently against Roan's knuckles, and something inside her begs for this to be more than kissing the ring. She can feel the adoration in Harrow's lips, in the tension in her fingers. But Roan wants it to be the kind of love she feels, returned in kind. She thinks about how there aren't enough words for the different kinds of love, not like other languages have, thinks about how there just might not be enough words, period, to explain the entirety of how she feels.

"I'll stay by your side as long as you'll have me," Harrow says.

But what about after this thing is born? Roan thinks, not knowing whether this question is her clawing towards some sort of solace or self-destruction. *After I am no longer holy, will you still worship me?*

The screen door opens again, derailing her thought, and a baby-faced young man in a skinny tie and a burly surfer blond with a camera on one shoulder and gear under his arm come out onto the back porch. They introduce themselves as Chris and Shaun and tell Roan she can sit still while they get set up.

"Weird," Shaun mutters to himself, looking at Roan through the camera after he sets it up on its tripod.

"Is everything okay?" Harrow asks, her concern obvious as Chris goes over to inspect.

"Weird, for sure," he says. Then, to Harrow, "No, yeah, it's fine, it's just..." He looks out into the fields, into the sky, back again. "She's already lit perfectly. And her makeup..." He examines Roan's face closely, looks between her and Harrow. "Do either of you have any experience in screen makeup or lighting?"

They both shake their heads.

"Huh," Chris says, shrugging. "Wonder if we can count this as our first miracle?" He says it with a laugh and a look over his shoulder at Shaun. Not deriding, but certainly not fully believing.

"So," Chris says, rubbing his hands together, "we ready to start?"

But before anyone can answer, the screen door bangs open yet again, and Paxton steps out onto the porch. He's holding his revolver at his hip, drawn, but not cocked, not pointed. As he leans against the doorway, more Pioneers appear, sauntering around the edges of the porch, appearing in the yard, boxing them in.

"Now, hold on before we really get into it," Paxton says, doing a slow turn and taking in everyone before him. "Things are gonna go a bit different than originally planned."

YOU CAN'T STOP THIS

"What do you think you're doing?" Harrow asks, moving to stand between Paxton and Roan. Roan notices this, sees the way Harrow spreads her stance out wide, her legs, her arms, making herself larger, protecting Roan.

It is true, she thinks. *She loves me.* But what kind of love is it? Does Harrow love her as a supplicant would love an idol, or as Roan has once loved?

"We're correcting this mistake, darlin'," Paxton says, "If everyone just remains calm, there's no need for anybody to get hurt."

Roan sees Chris nod to Shaun: *get all of this.*

"What's your plan?" Roan asks, surprised at the calm in her own voice. It isn't until she hears it aloud that she notices her heart isn't racing, that she's not hyperventilating. She's calm, calmer than she was when they took her to the barn. There's a certainty about her she cannot explain, a well of confidence pouring out of her, radiating from her stomach. The thing inside her knows.

Paxton raises his eyebrows at Roan over his wife's shoulder.

"Excuse me?"

"You heard me," Roan said, not leaving her chair. She's spoken up to men before, but not like this. Not with this absolute confidence. Before, she knew she'd have to back up such a claim with fists and teeth, if it came to that. And sometimes it did. But now she has something else, a weapon whose shape she can't define and yet knows she carries.

"What's your plan?" Roan narrows her eyes at Paxton, surprised at her own challenge. "You gonna cut the angel out of me?"

Paxton straightens. It looks like he's about to say something when Shaun chimes in, trying to break the tension.

"Look, everybody," he says, holding up his hands, camera abandoned. "Whatever this is, we don't need to get in the middle of it." He looks over to Chris, who in the last few moments has gone from dedicated newsman to fearing for his life. Things have escalated, become real in a way he is not prepared for. The presence of guns is one thing, but something has shifted in the air at Roan's challenge. They too must know that Paxton isn't a man who can let a challenge go unanswered.

"Too bad, son," Paxton says, moving the gun in his direction but not actually pointing it at him. The barrel is still below everyone's waists. "You're in the middle of it. Get the keys," he says to one of the Pioneers. A skinny guy in a baseball cap strides over and hits a button on the side of the camera and places the lens cap on it. Baseball Cap turns to Chris, holding out his hand, a wordless command, and Chris obeys.

"Paxton, stop this," Harrow says, continuing to plead with him, but her words go unheard.

"Round 'em all up," he says, and the surrounding Pioneers close in, pulling handcuffs from their belts like they're actually police, like they have any authority other than might. They grab Chris and Shaun, cuff them behind their backs. Chris briefly says something about being an American citizen, about having rights, but he swallows it when his eyes glance over all the guns, the body armor, the reflective sunglasses. Harrow struggles against a big, bearded Pioneer, pleading more with her words than her muscles, but they fall on deaf ears, Paxton watching her with something approaching pleasure.

Another Pioneer with the same edged cross tattoo as on the Columbia flag stands before Roan and simply holds out the open handcuffs. When she looks at him, she sees conflict on his face. He doesn't want to put his hands on a pregnant woman. He's young, confused, but he *wants* to feel sure. He wants to know what he's doing is right. His eyes plead with her, and Roan obliges him, lifting her hands so he can slide the cuffs over her wrists, cuffing her in front, whereas everyone else's hands are behind their backs. Cross Tattoo holds Roan by the elbow to help her stand.

"See?" Paxton asks everyone, sheathing his pistol. "Wasn't that easy?" He turns to lead the way out, and Roan addresses his back.

"You can't stop this."

Paxton turns back.

"What?"

Roan comes to her feet with Tattoo's help, but halfway there a pang hits her in the stomach, shakes her at the knees, and she grabs onto the young man for balance. She can't tell if this sudden pinch hurts or feels good, like the first time she ever slid a cock into her. It's both pain and pleasure, and she can't tell where the divide is, or if there even is one at all. She likes this feeling, wants more of it, at the same time wanting it to stop. Or maybe wanting the appearance of wanting it to stop. To say *no*, not the safe word.

Harrow crosses the porch to stand next to Roan, hands fidgeting uselessly behind her back.

"Roan, honey, are you all right?"

Roan sees the disgusted look Paxton gives his wife at seeing her hovering over another woman, and the sight of his pain gives her pleasure, the scales tipping.

"What's happening?" Harrow asks.

Roan doubles over, caught by both Tattoo and Baseball Cap, their chivalric instincts taking over, not allowing them to ignore a woman in distress on the distant chance that woman will return to them some sort of favor, hopefully sexual.

Their thoughts, Roan thinks. *Those were their thoughts.* She couldn't hear them, not like psychic people in the movies, but she could feel them. She was inside Tattoo and Baseball Cap's minds, feeling their loyalty to Paxton, not knowing what he was planning, and yet at the same time desiring to come to Roan's aid, for her to see them as strong, as worthy, as deserving of a reward. Even pregnant as she was, they imagined fucking her, lying on her side so her belly wouldn't get in the way.

That bolt of painful pleasure strikes Roan again, and she feels it decidedly move from her stomach down between her legs, and she suddenly pisses herself.

No.

Not piss. Not at all.

Roan feels a smile spread across her face as, doubled over, she looks down. A stream of yellow-brown fluid has splashed out of her and hit the porch. More of it continues to trickle down the insides of her thighs. She laughs, and that propels another large squirt out of her. She scrunches her toes, standing in the puddle of muck, as another wave hits her, and a third gush of fluid runs out of her, her body clenching, forcing it out.

From somewhere, Paxton screams a decidedly unmanly scream, and she can feel what he's thinking too, the disgust, the heresy that's running through his mind. It's not supposed to be like this, he thinks. Everything's gone wrong.

All around her, she can feel the Pioneers panicking, about to become witnesses to something they were told they'd never have to see—a deified version of what they were told was not appropriate for men, but only for the hidden lives of women. They share Paxton's revulsion.

"What's the matter?" Roan groans, looking up. Paxton stares down at her, a look of horror and disgust on his face. "You gonna ask me if I can hold it?" Paxton looks mortified, like he's about to hurl, and Roan thinks that it's just like a man to conflate being asked to step outside himself for even a single moment, to be asked to bear witness to the function of a woman's body with an assault on his freedoms, the end of the world. It's the face of a man who hasn't had to survive anything. Not like Roan has. Not like women have. Men don't have to be survivors in the same way. Men survive things like war, like earthquakes, like car accidents.

Women survive things like men.

RETURN

The Pioneers load them into separate trucks. They put Roan into the crew's van, along with Chris and Shaun. Baseball Cap drives, while Cross Tattoo sits in the back, a shotgun across his lap. Not pointed but present. Harrow is loaded into the backseat of Paxton's pickup, Paxton driving. Another Pioneer, this one with a gold hoop earring, looks back over the seat at her.

Harrow protests as she's separated from Roan, tries to fight back, to kick, but her efforts are useless with her hands behind her back.

"Don't worry," Roan says to Harrow, grunting as she's gripped by a contraction. How does this work, bringing this life into the world? It can't be the same as an ordinary child. She doesn't even have a womb. That can't really be a contraction that she feels. The Pioneers load her into the back of the van. "Everything's going to be all right."

The cold, hard slamming of the sliding door doesn't make Harrow think it will be, but she has to believe, has to have faith.

She's forced into the back of the truck.

"Where are we going?" Harrow asks as Paxton starts the truck and takes off ahead of the van.

"Back where it all started," he says, not even looking at her in the rearview mirror. "We're gonna go give this abomination back."

EPIPHANY

Roan leans back against Shaun, the big man offering the only help he can in their present condition. The van rumbles along behind Paxton's pickup, and Roan can think only of how she wants Harrow next to her for whatever is about to happen. More liquid spews out of her, across the floor of the van, and Roan feels a kind of intense relief and relaxation like finally pissing after holding it for a long time.

Is this it? she thinks. *This can't be it. It's supposed to hurt, isn't it?* She knows so, but then again, she only has a frame of reference for a biological birth, not for whatever is happening to her. Miracles are beyond her ken.

The men all try to keep their eyes averted, not knowing what to do or say. Nothing in their patriarchal—or in the case of the Pioneers, hypermasculine—upbringings has even remotely prepared them for this.

"We should turn around," Chris says, looking from Baseball Cap to Cross Tattoo and back again, but they show no emotion. "We gotta take her to a hospital." He looks down at the blood-tinged juices sloshing across the floor of the van and scooches away as it comes near him. Roan feels him notice a strange glint to it, like flakes of gold in the fluid. Whatever this is, it isn't normal. "We gotta take her to a hospital, guys. This is seriously fucked up."

"There's no hospital," Roan says, and she says it with a smile, "no hospital that can help with this." But her voice is hope*ful*, not hopeless. "They'll try to take it from me. Besides, it isn't for the rest of the world. Not yet."

Roan knows what she feels now, and it's not just peace. It's serenity.

"Shut up," Tattoo says, but without commitment, no edge in his voice. He too can tell this is wrong. He wants out. Roan can feel his thoughts.

"Are you all right?" Shaun asks Roan, looking down at her. It's a stupid question, an impossible question, but, strangely, she is. She lifts up her hands and touches her belly. She feels... light. Whatever it is, she can feel it coming, and she knows now that she isn't just a vessel for this force but a portal, something meant to bring so much more than a life into the world. She's meant to bring a revelation.

The small television monitor inside the van snaps to life.

Tattoo grips the shotgun.

"What?"

"I don't know," Chris says, looking around as if he can find the source of the disturbance. The television hisses nothing but scratchy static. "I don't know...."

The screen slowly comes to life, an image coming into focus, still scratchy and grainy like it was recorded on an old VHS.

Three enormous crosses sitting atop a hill.

"What the fuck?" Shaun mutters.

Roan holds her belly tight, feeling the warmth coming not from her but from whatever's inside her, pushing its way into the world, and she begins opening herself up to let it in.

"I don't like this," Tattoo says, turning away from the screen to look at Roan. "Are you doing this?" he asks her. "Stop doing this!"

Roan says nothing to him, only smiles. Another spike of something hits between her legs, and she can feel it moving now, coming, getting ready for its grand entrance. Its revelation.

"Make it stop," Tattoo says, gripping the shotgun tighter. He hasn't turned it on her yet, but Roan can tell it's coming any second now and knows he'll be sorry when it does. "Turn it off!" Tattoo shouts, finally pointing the shotgun, finally firing like he's threatened to, even though Roan can see in his eyes he's just as surprised as everyone else.

But Roan, she pushes. Not as a pregnant woman pushes, but feeling the energy inside her, the force crawling its way out into the world, and she moves on instinct, some sort of vestigial memory, listening to her body in the moment, and she directs that energy. The shotgun discharges, but not with pellets. No, there's instead a fast-motion explosion of vibrant color—greens and reds and even bright browns. A tree explodes its way out of the shotgun, its leaves filling the inside of the truck, its branches striking the driving Baseball Cap on the side of the head and knocking him into the steering wheel, bursting forth out of the windows, shattering the glass, snapping themselves on the steel interior of the truck when they have nowhere else to go.

The van lurches forward and slams into the back of Paxton's truck.

THE GREAT DIVORCE

Harrow feels the van collide with the truck. She doesn't know why or what could have happened to cause it, but she doesn't wait, doesn't question. She holds on as the truck's tires spin, failing to catch the dirt road. They go sailing off into the plain, and someone's gun goes off—she doesn't know whose. Harrow knows she's hurt, but she doesn't know if she's shot, even as the truck sails through the air, over bumps and rocks, ditches, into and through prairie dog holes, and finally comes to a stop slamming into a large boulder, the front crumpling.

She doesn't lose consciousness. She lifts her head up, tries to look out the windshield, but it's shot through with cracks and covered in blood. There's a sick gurgle to her right, and she sees the Pioneer that came with them with a bullet hole in his neck. He breathes, and the hole gushes blood, each pump losing pressure.

His revolver is free, on the floor in front of her, barrel smoking.

"Harrow," Paxton calls from the front seat. She looks up and sees him in the dangling rear-view mirror, a leaking wound on his forehead. "Don't move." He pulls his hand up to the wound, staunching the blood flow. Of course, he managed to hold onto his gun. He waves it around, swaying in his seat, and Harrow knows she has to move.

She reaches for the loose pistol and snatches it before Paxton can stop her. She elbows him in her panic—she's not quite sure where, and it doesn't matter where; she just needs to stun him—as she leans across the seat to grab the keys out of the ignition. Yanks them free. Sees the tiny nub of the handcuff key dangling from the ring.

"Don't!" Paxton slurs, trying to reach for her. Harrow yanks back, but he has her by the hair, his grip iron and bloody. He pulls her close, and she can smell the blood on his face, feel it in her nose and mouth. "Don't you walk away fr—!" he growls but is interrupted as Harrow slams her closed fists and the butt of the pistol into his face. It's unprotected, one hand on her, the other at the wound at the side of his head, and she hits him so hard his head bounces off the driver's window with a dull echo.

Harrow pushes the door open and slides through a sheet of broken glass, ignoring the pain, pushing through, stumbling out into the desert. She hits the ground and crawls through the dust, away from Paxton's truck, freeing herself from the handcuffs as she goes. She tosses them away and finally pulls herself to her feet, looking back the way they'd come.

And she sees it.

The tree.

The television crew's van is in the road, its roof burst open, and from the inside of the van sprouts an enormous tree unlike any she's seen before, limbs stretching toward the sky. The trunk and roots are hidden inside the van, but she can see thick, ripe fruits dangling from the branches, pink like budding strawberries, fruits whose beautiful skins catch the sun, making them look like miniature stars. The tree stands against the blue sky like a monolith, pure, white clouds cutting behind it, those pink fruits gleaming.

Harrow shakes her head, but the tree is still there. It hasn't left, isn't a figment of her imagination, and then she remembers where she is and what's happening, and she stumbles towards the tree, towards Roan.

ABANDONED

Paxton feels Harrow slip through his grip, from his sight. All he's left with is a bleeding corpse in the front seat. The Pioneer takes a final, sucking breath before his head lolls down onto his chest and he stops moving.

Paxton reminds himself to say a small prayer later, to give the kid some sort of remembrance, but now he has more important things to do. He reaches down to the door and with some effort he opens it, chasing his wife out into the road.

APOTHEOSIS

The sliding door of the van is open, and Roan sits on the edge, ass and swollen belly hanging over, feet on the dirt road. She grits her teeth and pushes, expelling a stream of milky fluid out into the dirt. She expects this to smell, but instead it's sweet. Like honey. Little golden flakes flicker inside it. The expulsion hurts, but it feels wonderful. It feels like something's coming alive, like after this moment, the world will be fundamentally changed. And it will be.

You're almost here.

"Roan!" She looks up at the sound of her name and sees Harrow coming around the side of the van, a six-shooter in her right hand. "I'm here! I'm here!" She skids to a stop in front of Roan, heedless of the puddle between her feet, only hesitating as she looks up at the enormous tree that's taken root behind her. Roan knows what Harrow sees, the same thing she herself saw as she rolled halfway out of the van—the trunk of the tree stretching up towards the sky, those heavy, ripe fruits dangling above them like precious planets. The tree's trunk cuts through the floor of the van and directly into the dirt below, as if it had been growing there for generations and the van had the audacity to get in its way. The limbs of one of the branches pierced the back of Baseball Cap's skull and went all the way out through the windshield, impaling him in place. The back doors of the van were blown open in the crash, Roan sees the reporters and Cross Tattoo lying in the middle of the road.

Cross tries to get up, but Harrow puts him down with a bullet just to the left of his nose when he reaches for his holstered pistol. His brain and skull hit the pavement, sizzling in the heat. The reporters scream, and the smaller one vomits onto the side of the road.

Harrow crouches down before Roan and holds her by the shoulders, lowers her forehead to hers. "Are you okay?" she pants. "I can't believe I just did that. Are you okay?"

Roan looks up into Harrow's eyes.

"I am now."

"I won't let anything happen to you." Harrow laughs.

Gunshots cut through the moment.

Harrow and Roan both jump, and though neither of them feels the pain of the bullet, they each feel it whiz by them, superheating the air.

"God-fucking—" Paxton growls as he stumbles into the road, one hand holding his pistol, the other clapped to the side of his head. His nose is gushing blood, and there must be some wound on his back or the back of his head, Roan guesses, by the way the back of his shirt is soaked. She can see it as he wobbles, trying to hold himself upright. There's blood all over his face, in his eyes, and he's trying to level the gun at Harrow or Roan—it's impossible to tell.

Harrow is faster.

She shoots Paxton in the stomach, doubling him over and dropping him to the ground. She rises, and as Paxton attempts to pull his gun up, she shoots him again. The large caliber slug bursts forth out of the chamber and smashes into the side of Paxton's firearm. It blazes a furrow down the inside of his gun, shearing off his index and middle fingers and a chunk of his thumb as it cuts through the air, blasting through his wrist and burying itself in the dirt behind him. It is a one-in-a-million shot, one Roan knows Harrow could never have made meaning to, and she feels the angel's will inside her again.

He needs to see, Roan thinks, though she isn't entirely sure if it's in the angel's voice or her own. *He will be the first witness.*

Paxton hits the dirt screaming, and Harrow rushes over and kicks his gun away into the roadside ditch, keeping her own pistol trained on Paxton's head.

"God, you bitch," he spits into the dirt. "You shot me, you fucking bitch!"

"Don't move," she says.

He will be the first witness, and then they will all be witnesses.

Roan can't see, but she can feel the reporters fumbling with their camera, more out of desperation, pure fear in an attempt to preserve their lives, than with a devotion to getting the shot.

"Harrow!" Roan shouts.

Harrow looks over her shoulder and sees Roan kneeling in the middle of the road, gripping the side of the van with one hand and her belly with the other. Harrow leaves her husband and rushes back to Roan's side while keeping her gun trained on him. Roan reaches out and grabs her, and Harrow takes her shoulder. "It's happening." She looks up into Harrow's eyes, her own gushing with tears of both pain and happiness, her mouth a wide, anticipatory smile. "Tell me. Please tell me."

Harrow drops her pistol and takes Roan's head in her hands. She reaches down and kisses Roan on the lips, hard, with feeling, and then a longer, more tender one on the forehead.

"You can do this," she says. "You're so strong." And it's like her words finally give Roan permission. Roan feels a part of herself split open. Not her body, but her soul. She rips in half as she expels whatever is inside her out and into the world. She can feel it coming even though she knows it's not her corporeal form that's the portal, at least not entirely.

Across the road, Paxton cannot resist the temptation. Like Lot's wife. He looks when he knows he shouldn't. He tears his gaze away from his wife, from the strange tree, and looks at Roan. He does, in fact, bear witness to the opening of the portal, to the apotheosis, the arrival of something new and—for him—terrible. The angel breaches into the world and what Paxton sees is too much for him. His mind collapses. A kaleidoscope of color and terror he can only barely comprehend is his final image as a wash of pink and blue light hits him and vaporizes him, leaving him nothing more than a vaguely human-shaped stain on a nearby boulder.

Chris and Shaun, though, are spared. They see the light through the screen of the camera, and it's beautiful. They do indeed bear witness. Everyone witnesses, as they beam the images captured onscreen out into the world.

Roan's cosmic contractions peak in a surge of pain and electricity, and she knows without a doubt she shits herself like the Virgin Mary probably shit herself, and it's the most beautiful thing in a world that is now irrevocably changed.

THE PARENTS OF GOD

It is easy to deify a thing in this world. To bring it up to the level of a god. Humans have made gods of money, war, sex, death. Obsessions over millennia coming back over and over again. But what would something beyond human deify? What is always deified?

Parents.

Children. They are always more than they could ever be.

The child that is born in the desert outside Parthas, Nevada, looks up at its parents, two women, and as they gaze down upon it, think-ing—knowing—that it is a god beyond this world, the child thinks the same of them. That they are deities, and they are to be protected at all costs. In time, it will do what all children will do at one point or another, take its worldview from its parents. And because it is a god, because it has been deified, it will have the power to make that worldview a reality.

It will be a neon revelation upon humanity.

Acknowledgements

Writing this book was a blast, but editing it was a bit of an angry slog. A lot changed in the world between the time I first wrote this story and its publication, and a lot in the story changed with it. A lot of it was funny sacrilegious poops at first, but now much more of it is rage. Sylvia and Timber Ghost Press were there for the latter half, and a huge thank you has to go out to them for fighting through every single day of existence under a regime that wants to see us annihilated. Thank you for letting me make this story even angrier and queerer before we even started the official editing process. A big sorry to my parents for what you just read. Big thanks to my Horror Writer Group and the GTTUnit for being there for advice and support, and to my wife for sitting with me through all my tonal hyperfixations whenever I'm deep in a writing project.

ABOUT THE AUTHOR

TT Madden (they/them) is a genderfluid, mixed-race author of weird fiction who refuses to keep "politics" out of their writing and to put AI in. When they're not exploring the woods around their home looking for spooky inspiration, they can be found on Instagram, Bluesky, and TikTok as @ttmaddenwrites, and at ttmaddenwrites.carrd.co.

A NOTE FROM TIMBER GHOST PRESS

I f you enjoyed *The Neon Revelation*, please consider leaving a review on Amazon or Goodreads. Reviews help the authors and the press.

If you go to www.timberghostpress.com you can sign up for our newsletter so you can stay up-to-date on all our upcoming titles, plus you'll get informed of new horror flash fiction and poetry featured on our site monthly.

Take care and thanks for reading *The Neon Revelation!*

-Timber Ghost Press